The Price of Loyalty

From the Historian Tales

By Lance Conrad

To Alexis,

[signature]

4-7-21

DawnStar
PRESS

The following is a work of fiction. All names, places, characters and events portrayed herein are the invention of the author's imagination or are used fictitiously. Any similarity to any real persons or occurrences is purely coincidental.

The Price of Loyalty

ISBN: 978-0-9910230-5-9

Printed in the United States of America

For my daughter,
who gives me joy

Chapter 1

I am the Historian. I am immortal. I am ageless. I am nameless. I am carried by my own feet through times and worlds to witness great stories.

This is one such story.

This story is hard for me to tell.

Distance, time, life and death all become fuzzy concepts when the numbers get high enough and a certain detachment naturally evolves. Simply put, I've seen it all and I've seen it so many times that nothing is that special any more. That is what makes this story stand out more than any other.

This one is personal.

I was shaken right from the beginning. There was nothing noticeable about the day or anything in it, merely another light ebb in the passage of time.

I heard a strange noise and moved to investigate. It crackled and whooshed, the sound of wind and heat. It reminded me of a forest fire, though I could see no smoke in the sky. Neither did I sense the panic of animals that usually accompanies that kind of catastrophe. It was enough for a closer look.

More than that, it had been a long time since I had run into anyone at all. It wasn't that odd to walk for years, even decades, without meeting another human being, but even a Historian can feel loneliness.

I suppose, in a way, Historians can never stop feeling a little lonely. Suffice it to say, even if there was no great story, I was anxious to hear a voice that was not my own.

I simply wasn't ready for what that voice had to say.

I topped the crest of a hill and witnessed a battle of magic unfolding below me. It was two men, both dressed in rough leather. Rage and hate coursed over their faces as they hurled elemental magic at one another. Unnatural fire spouted from their hands, battering at each other like hammers, though I noticed that their burns weren't as serious as they should have been.

One man, with wild gray hair, rolled away from an attack and fired back one of his own in a focused beam of flame. It struck the other man in the eyes and he fell to his knees, crying out in pain. Whatever protection he enjoyed had failed him and the wild-looking man moved to press his advantage.

He rushed at the man, but rather than using more magic to finish him off, he scooped up a large rock from the ground and threw it overhand as soon as he was within range. The rock struck the other man in the chest and drove him onto his back, gasping.

I found myself suddenly too close. Having been away from people for so long, my sensitivities were dulled and I found myself walking closer and closer, carelessly, like a moth drawn to a flame of violence.

I was close enough to see madness flash in the eyes of the first man as he came to stand over his fallen opponent. I was so near I could see the spots of char that dotted his rough leathers, as well as the burn scars that marred his own hide.

2

He knelt down and put both hands on the other man who was still gasping for air after the rock had pounded his chest. There was a momentary flash of light and the man on the ground arched his back for a shadow of a second before lying still, the life gone from his body.

The victor staggered to his feet, exhausted. I had no idea how long the two men had battled or what this form of magic took from its user. If there was one thing I knew about the universe, it was that you didn't get something for nothing. Whether it was magic, science, or pure human will, there was always a cost associated with changing something in the world.

He rubbed his knuckles at his eyes and he looked for a moment like a man about to cry. A vast weariness weighed down on him and it looked like he might fall back to the ground at any moment. Then he lifted his head and saw me.

His expression of fatigue and sadness vanished in the first blink. The second blink encompassed confusion and disbelief, then that vanished. Both flashes of emotion were drowned out in a wave of fury and disgust. Flames licked around his hands and he shot them out at me and followed them up with a shouted curse.

"Historian!"

The word, spat from his mouth like bile, oozed with contempt and fear. The flames from his hands rolled over me and I cringed from some ancient instinct, crouching to protect myself from flames that couldn't have hurt me.

When I straightened back up, feeling a little sheepish, the man was gone. If I had been thinking straight, I would have sat and waited.

The man couldn't have gone far, even with magic. If I had been patient, he would have eventually moved from his hiding place and I could have asked him some questions about what had happened.

As it was, I was not thinking clearly. It was the first and only time that I had ever been recognized for who I was. I had worn so many names and titles that I could scarcely remember all of them or even distinguish between them any longer.

The only thing I truly knew for sure was that none of them were my real name. I could feel that space inside me. I knew I was a Historian, but I did not know how I knew. Thousands of years had dulled my curiosity and I didn't even question it anymore. Rather, I embraced the one fact of my existence I could lay hold on.

Now here was a man who knew at a glance who and what I was. Thousands of questions roared through my head with all the intensity that comes with long repression. I took off walking towards the place where he had been standing. There was nothing on the ground but scorch marks from the vicious battle. There was no clue as to who the men were or why they had been fighting.

A brief investigation of the dead man gave me no more clues. He carried nothing on him but scars, similar to those of the man who had left.

His clothes were that of a hermit or madman. Rough leather had holes cut in it and the edges were tied together with strands of sinew to make a rough covering. The man who left had been wearing the same thing. If I had come upon this them without seeing what had happened, I would have thought these men only a short step above animals, closer to cavemen than masters of magic.

Still, I could not deny the intelligence behind the eyes I had seen, even with all the other emotions that had raged in them.

I took a quick survey of the land. I had to find this man again and find out what he knew. He might know something I didn't know myself, not that it would take much.

I walked as I thought through the situation, moving towards the notches I could see cut in the mountains. I had no special powers and I couldn't tell the future, but with enough experience, one can decipher the patterns well enough.

I broke down what I knew. The man was clearly a magic user of great skill. Someone like that couldn't remain anonymous. The mere fact that I found him in the middle of a fight suggested that conflict raged in this land.

All that remained to me was to find the closest town or city and ask around. Finding people is always easy. People follow patterns more than any other animal, though they tend to see it least of all. You could always count on people to set up their civilizations right around water. Even nomadic tribes charted their routes from one water source to another.

Advanced societies that were no longer dependent on natural water sources still tended to stick close to where their ancestors had first settled.

My first step was to find water, which was why I was heading to the cleft in the mountains. I could see mountains for hundreds of miles and see where they have been cut by millions of years of running water.

I headed towards such a place now. I would find the river, then follow it down into the valley. If there wasn't a town on that river, I would skip to the next one until I had found someone.

I could not remember a time I had felt so determined. I was driven to find this man of fire who knew the closest thing I had to a name.

I realized as I walked how deeply his reaction bothered me. There was more to it than recognition. The man had hated me. I knew nothing of my life before becoming a Historian, but while I had pondered endlessly about family, friends, and adventures I might have had, I never considered that I might have enemies, powerful enemies.

My thoughts flew and so did my feet. In no time at all I breathed sweet mountain air. It was clear and cold and smelled of pines. Cutting across the hills, I found running water. It wasn't much of a river, but no rivers are at their headwaters. I stooped down and took a drink.

I can't say why I did that.

While I certainly have the ability, I don't have any particular need to eat or drink. I think I had started getting nostalgic. If that man knew me, then perhaps this is the world from which I came.

This could be home.

I coursed my way down the mountain with the waters of the river. The little stream grew larger and stronger as other small streams and tributaries silently folded themselves in. I slowed my walk, just a little, to breathe deeply of the sweet air.

Then my nose caught a whiff of something else. Wood smoke. My step quickened again, eager to find someone I could talk to about the strange sorcerer I had encountered.

Muddy footsteps on the bank showed that someone had left the river here and went in a straight line away from the water. Some distant part of my mind noted the strange nature of the footprints. They were deep, deeper than they should have been, and they were erratic, as if whoever it was had been struggling to walk.

Still, footprint subtleties were the farthest thing from my mind as I chased off in the direction they led. The prints were still fresh, they couldn't have been more than a couple hours old.

I didn't have far to walk before a beautiful cultivated field opened up before me. Golden stalks of grain swayed softly in the breeze, undulating with the wind like a dancer.

A small house presided over the field from the far end of the clearing. A wispy trail of smoke wound its way heavenward from the chimney. That must have been what I smelled back by the river. Whoever had made the footprints had walked straight through the field. Broken and crushed stalks combined to suggest a muddy trail that cut awkwardly through the field. I followed suit.

Seconds before I broke through the edge of the field, it finally dawned on me that I had no idea how I would start a conversation like the one I needed to have. There were a lot of pitfalls with each new land and culture. If I wasn't careful, I could find myself in a lot of trouble.

The thought slowed me down. My Historian patience finally reasserted itself in my mind. There was too much at stake here for me to rush this. I was in no hurry, after all. I needed to understand the situation a little more before I started sticking my nose in.

I shook my head to clear it and assumed my regular pose of a meandering traveler possibly looking for a meal or a bed. It was a persona I had down perfectly. It was the ideal blend of badly disguised eagerness and an affected nonchalance.

Chapter 2

It is impossible for the sane to truly understand madness.
–Musings of the Historian

My theatrics were wasted. The man who sat on the front
porch didn't even look my way as I walked up. His eyes were fixed
on some point in the distance.

Tears ran freely down his face, though there was nothing
else to suggest that he was crying. There was no look of sadness,
sound of sobbing, or trembling in the shoulders. There were only
lonely trails of wetness building to drips along his jaw.

I coughed, feeling awkward, uninvited to this emotional
moment. He swung his head to look at me and squinted a bit as he
looked me up and down.

"Now isn't a good time, whoever you are." His lifeless voice
dismissed me and he looked back to his imaginary vision. My
curiosity about the man I had seen out in the country faded as my
compassion was stirred for this man. Whatever my problems, it
seemed that this poor soul had it worse.

"Is there something I can do to help?" I offered. He shook his
head slowly, as if the motion hurt him, though he was clearly
uninjured.

"Would you tell me about it?" I pressed. The hopeless always have an urge to share their story. It's as if having someone know of their struggle somehow gives it meaning. I suppose it does, in a way.

"Who are you?" The sad eyes were on me again. It was hard to say for sure with the emotions laying heavy on his features, but he looked to be around forty years old. Powerful shoulders and callused hands told the story of a lifetime of hard labor.

Men like him were the salt of the earth. They would never be rich or famous. They would die one day in the fields with their legacy around them in the dirt. They were the shapers of land. They were the ancestors.

"I'm just a traveler. I have come from far away and wanted to hear another human voice. I've been getting on my own nerves."

"If you want stories and gossip, you should keep walking. The village is another couple miles further down the river. There's nothing I can offer you here."

I nearly took him up on his offer, but something stopped me. An itch at the back of my mind told me there was a story here. It wasn't much, like a push from a feather, but after so long, I felt it easily.

I rationalized that any great story would eventually include fearsome people, like the man I sought. In my mind, I settled in for the long haul. I edged my way forward and sat down on the porch with the man, though not so close as to make it uncomfortable for him.

"Perhaps there is something I can offer you," I suggested, looking for an opening. He raised his hands in refusal.

"If you're a peddler, you're really wasting your time. We have no money and nothing we can spare. I do all the work here. We can't afford and don't need another hand. Perhaps you'd better be on your way."

I really only had one card left to play, though I had to be careful how I went about it.

"All right, I'll be on my way, but before I go, I was wondering if you could tell me something. I saw something... strange, on my way here. Do you know of anything going on that could be of danger to travelers?"

"Hmph!" he snorted. I had hit a nerve at last. "You don't need to travel to be in danger. There is plenty to be had, even for those who do nothing at all."

"I'm not sure I follow you, friend. Are you in danger?"

Tears welled again in his eyes.

"No, not me."

I about had him broken now. I made my final move, carefully putting the final crack in the dam.

"So then, someone you care about. Can't you protect them?"

It was a bit of a low blow, I have to admit. It was obvious the poor man had no chance at relief. Such a question would only serve to rub salt into an open wound. He shuddered as if struck. The dam broke and the words came rushing out in a flood of frustration and bitterness.

"How can I protect someone from themselves? Twenty years I have protected her. I have shielded her from the cold, the heat, famine and violence. Look at this, this scar. I got that fighting a wolf who got into the stock. Why couldn't it be like that?

"I am still strong. I have wronged no man. Why now am I faced with a battle I can't win? Why?"

10

His voice broke at this last agonized word. It was the primal question of intelligent beings. As an animal writhes in pain, so a thinking mind squirms under uncertainty and injustice.

It was obvious that this man was not usually an emotional person, he wasn't the type. The heavy emotions he struggled under fit him poorly, like an overlarge hat. He had been worn down over a long period of time. Even the strongest of characters can be worn down and broken with enough time and pressure.

My eyes wandered over him, searching for more clues, and took note of the mud on his pants. In fact, most of his clothes were sopping wet, though their color didn't make it immediately obvious. My mind shot back to the riverbank, the uneven footprints, too deep in the mud. Everything started to click together and then I had it.

"She tried to drown herself, didn't she? You pulled her out."

Once broken down, the walls don't go back up quickly. He nodded, confirming my suspicions.

"This is the second time she's tried it. I've locked up everything in the house that has an edge to it, but there's nothing I can do. I'm only putting it off. How can you save someone so determined to end themselves?"

"What made her so sad? Did she lose someone?"

It's a sad fact that things often go wrong with small farms like this. Even with every precaution, children could be swept away by nothing more than an exceptionally cold night. A grieving mother might get swallowed up by her loss and choose to follow her child to the grave, especially if it were her only one.

"Nothing like that. It's the madness."

This was the infuriating part about always being new to an

area, everyone used the terms they were familiar with and expected you to know them as well. Still, there was nothing for it. You had to jump in, ask the obvious questions and have people look at you like you're some kind of simpleton.

"What kind of madness? I have encountered many people with afflictions of the mind. Could you tell me the symptoms?"

The expected look of disbelief was right on cue.

"I hope you don't feign ignorance to mock me, traveler. There are many ways that people can lose touch with reality, but there is only one madness."

"I am certainly not mocking you, good sir," I said in a comforting tone, sensitive to his raw emotions. "I simply would like to know specifically what is happening to your..."

I was stuck. I knew it was a female, but for a man of this age, it could be wife, daughter, mother, or sister. Luckily, my obvious unease and sudden stuttering helped convince him of my sincerity. He spoke up and saved me.

"It is my wife that is afflicted. Her name is Edana." Something in the way he said the word "wife" set something off in my mind, but I filed it away for later questioning and leaned forward to listen to his explanation.

"She started almost a year ago. She has already lasted longer than most. People with the madness inevitably end their own lives. They are unable to bear what it does to their minds. Some disappear in the night and are never seen again."

"What does it do to their minds?" I knew it was a touchy subject, so I tried to keep things general, not specific to his wife.

"They break down. Something inside them starts to wear

away, like a riverbank. It starts with an irritability, they yell at people for no reason. That isn't much, but it's only the beginning. It gets worse and worse.

"Eventually they become violent, and there is a madness in it. My wife broke her favorite vase, a white delicate thing that had been her mother's. She stood over it and stomped on it over and over again. When her boots could do no more damage, she grabbed a hammer and spent the next hour there on the floor, crushing each piece to dust.

"Rather than providing relief, it made things worse. When there was nothing left of it to break, she pounded on the dust with her fists and screamed at it, her face wet with tears. That was two months ago.

"Now the only things left in the house are things she can't break, though heaven knows she tries. Even the walls have been gouged by her nails. She has become like a caged beast."

There was no denying the hopelessness of the situation. Whatever this affliction was, it happened often enough that people knew its full progression.

What he described was tragic enough, but it was even worse to consider what hadn't been said. No mention at all had been made of any sort of treatment or survival. This madness, whatever it was, was a death sentence. A slow death that dragged every loved one down with it.

This was a strong man, and he clearly loved his wife; though in his description, I again noted the strange tone he used when he said "wife." But for all his strength and love, he was all but broken, a shattered child in a man's body.

Impulsively, I reached out and put my hand on his shoulder. It was a comforting gesture in nearly every culture I had visited and it seemed the only appropriate response to his description of utter despair. Of course, there was one land where the gesture was a vile insult and a challenge, but that was a rare exception in a culture that took respect for personal space to an unhealthy extreme.

He looked at me and nodded, acknowledging my effort, but the depression didn't waver even for a moment.

"Does she recognize you? Or does the madness destroy all of the mind?"

"She knows me." His tone didn't make it sound like good news. "It is as if her mind is alive and healthy, but there is something else in there taking over. She has cursed me and apologized in the same breath. Sometimes she even apologizes first.

"That ended about a month ago. She doesn't truly speak anymore. She only screams now, incoherent screeches no one could understand."

"I am truly sorry for this sickness that has taken your wife. If I might be bold, what do you plan to do?"

The question sparked something and he was angry all at once, turning to face me, fists clenched.

"I don't like what you're suggesting, stranger. I won't do it! I can't kill her!"

"No, no, no!" I stammered trying to defuse the situation. "I didn't mean any such thing! Do people do that?"

His face softened, though his fists remained clenched.

"Yes, they say it is a mercy. The law has no penalty for killing someone with the madness." His fists unclenched and his whole body relaxed with them. "Perhaps they are right. Her existence must be something horrible for her to want to end her own life. She was always so strong."

"Logic and reason don't count for much when it comes to raising your hand against someone you love. I understand why you can't do it, I don't think I could do such a thing."

Actually, I had no idea. Such decisions were made by people living their lives. My life was observation. I watched other people make these choices. Still, my words had their planned effect and he mumbled his gratitude, once again fighting back tears.

"What is your name?"

"My name is Altur. What's yours?"

Once again, I froze. It was the one question I truly couldn't answer. I should have avoided it, steered the conversation away from names. Instead, I had walked right into it.

Normally, I would work around it, or ask my host to pick a name for me, but Altur wasn't in any shape for naming or elusive explanations.

I needed to give him a name, any name.

I wracked my brain. Thousands of names flowed through my memory, each one tied to a story. Each time I opened my mouth to say one of them, my tongue seized and I couldn't do it. I couldn't claim a name that wasn't my own.

The effect was one of a fish, mouth opening and closing in an awkward rhythm. Altur was distracted from his own troubles long enough to stare at me curiously. His mind likely went to my comment about other sicknesses of the mind.

Necessity is truly the mother of invention, and I rolled the dice with a gambit.

"The Historian," I said. But I didn't quite say it like that. I mumbled it softly and cleared my throat, as if a bug had flown into my mouth halfway through. I also wiped my forearm across my mouth as I said it, just for good measure. Altur's confused look held for a second longer, then he took a stab at it.

"Your name is Tory?"

I smiled broadly.

"It's a fine name, isn't it? I am glad to meet you, Altur. I wish it were under better circumstances."

"Good meeting to you as well, Tory, and no one wishes that more than I."

We shared a moment of silence, looking out at the lush golden field. I still had that itch, the instinct that there was more of a story here than the tragedy of a woman gone mad. I hazarded my old question again.

"So what do you plan to do? Is there anything that can be done to help her?"

"There is nothing. I cannot take her life, and there is no relief for what ails her. All I can do is keep her from killing herself. Luckily, she stills eats and drinks. She does it automatically, like she doesn't know she's doing it. Maybe there is something left of her.

"Maybe if I can wait this out long enough, the madness will find an end. Maybe she can learn to be herself again."

It was a fool's hope and we both knew it. Degenerative diseases didn't turn around all by themselves. They seldom did it with treatment. Unable to help myself, I nudged him toward this reality.

16

"Hasn't anyone tried that before? Have any of the others shown an improvement?"

New tears gave me my answer.

"What else can I do? I cannot kill her and I cannot stand by and let her kill herself. No one has ever died of the madness. They either kill themselves or disappear forever."

"No one has found the ones that disappear?"

"No, but that is expected with the madness. They would flee so that they could kill themselves, away from anyone who would try to stop them. If they drowned in a river, which seems to be the most common method, the current could carry them endless miles into the badlands, far beyond where we could send a search party."

"I guess there is nothing else you can do," I admitted. His shoulders slumped a little more to have his fears acknowledged and confirmed. He looked to me with the desperation of a drowning man.

"Would you wait and watch with me?"

"What?" I knew what he was asking and I stalled to think it over.

"Please. Surely you are tired from the road and could use a place to stay for a while. She has only become worse. I do everything I can, but after all I can do, I still have to rest. That is how she got down to the river this time. I was too exhausted and I fell asleep, thinking that she was also sleeping. But it was the madness, a moment of silence before an attack.

"Please stay with me. With two of us, taking turns, perhaps we can make it longer than those others. Surely you wouldn't deny me this one chance at hope."

His one chance at hope was a wandering stranger that happened upon his land. That alone told me how far gone hope was for this man. Still, he was right about one thing. I couldn't deny him the chance.

Chapter 3

Never underestimate a farmer.
–Musings of the Historian

I nodded my assent and his rough, heavy hand reached over to clasp mine. For a reserved man like that, the clasped hand was the equivalent of a tight embrace and tears on my shoulder.

I was grateful for his restraint.

When the moment ended, he showed me around the farm. It was a nice little place. The buildings were old, but kept in good repair by knowing hands. The fields had been carefully worked and he showed me another couple fields that were farther from this little meadow.

I admired the experience this farmer displayed as he motioned to fields left fallow to let the nutrients build back up in the soil.

Too many farmers would plant all the land they could, trying to milk all profit from the dirt. In a few years, they would rant and pull at their hair when their crops started to produce less and less.

The pinnacle of our little tour was when he showed me the inside of the house. As he had said, all furniture had been removed. Marks on the walls showed the scars of former fits.

It didn't take much imagination to complete the image of the afflicted woman throwing chairs and heaving tables in her rage.

For the moment, she lay peacefully in sleep, no trace of fury marked her features. She was a pretty woman, in her own wholesome way. A hint of freckles was barely visible on her tanned face, a light dusting across the nose. Her face was almond-shaped, with soft skin and a feminine chin.

Soft brown hair gathered under her head like a pillow. Small ripples of muscle were visible in her arms, even as she slept. This woman was used to hard work, like her husband.

That is what it took in situations like this. There wasn't a choice. Everyone worked as long and as hard as they were able. To do anything else would be to tempt fate, and fate enjoys punishing the careless with freeze and famine.

Even with the signs of hard labor evident on her body, she was still young, quite a bit younger than Altur. I glanced back over to him and saw him gazing down at his wife.

The look on his face was distilled tenderness. It was true, I thought to myself, there was no way in this world that Altur would ever be capable of raising his hand to kill this woman. It was a look that said that her mere discomfort was a pain to him.

The utter hopelessness of their situation moved me to the core. I knew in that moment that I would not leave this man until the story had ended, though I could only imagine tragedy. Little did I know then how much of the tragedy would be my own.

The tour over, Altur apologized profusely, but begged me to stand watch at the door while he went and got some sleep in the barn. She had been raving all through the previous night and much of the morning, and he had stayed with her until she quieted. I agreed and ushered him off to take his rest.

I sat on the front porch and waited. At one juncture, she woke up and screamed at the door for an hour before her voice gave out and she pounded at the door with her fists. There was nothing for it, though. Altur had switched the bar to lock from the outside and permanently sealed the back door. She was imprisoned, a beast in a cage, like Altur had said.

You might think that this was a traumatic experience for me, sitting guard while a mad woman raged and hurt herself a couple feet away. While it reflects badly on me as a person, I have to admit that after the first couple minutes, I tuned her out and went back to contemplating the wind in the fields.

Experience brings calm, and I was more experienced than anyone. There was even something strangely comforting having someone so alive close by, after all the time I had spent alone on this last walk.

When her voice gave out, she settled down to hitting something against the floor. Since there was nothing else in the house, I was forced to conclude that she must have been hitting the floor with some part of her own body, her head or hands.

In time, even that stopped and there was silence again. She must have worn herself out. No madness will ever truly triumph over fatigue. In the end, the body demands that the mind shut down for a while.

At last, Altur emerged from the barn, looking much more

like a man. His shoulders were squared and his steps were long and confident. It's amazing the difference a little sleep and someone to share your struggle with can make.

Altur took care of everything. He worked the fields, he made all the meals, and he saw to Edana's every need. He didn't let me help with anything else and heaped praise and gratitude on me for my role, which turned out to be watching Edana while he slept.

It suffices to say that things slipped into a kind of pattern and held steady for a solid month. The only thing that changed over that time was Edana's state of mind. It grew steadily worse and Altur had to force her to wear leather mittens that he strapped onto her wrists so she couldn't take them off. This was so she couldn't scratch at herself or him when he entered to take care of her.

With regular sleep and someone to talk to, Altur's courage did not break again like it had on the day I met him. He calmly adapted to each new development in his wife. There was no more talk about killing or giving up, only a steady plod through each new day.

From my own perspective, any sliver of hope there might have been when I showed up had long since vanished. There was certainly no improvement and her affliction got worse by the day.

Calling her behavior animal-like no longer did it justice. After all, even animals have their moments of serenity. All such times were gone for Edana. I didn't know how much longer this could go on.

Then came the night when everything changed.

I was in the barn, "sleeping." Altur insisted on taking the night shifts, as they were often the worst. Any excuses I made about not needing much sleep were waved aside and he insisted that I go sleep. So I would go to the barn, shut the door, and wait for eight hours or so, feeling a little silly.

On that night, my simulated slumber was interrupted by screaming.

"NO, NO, NO!" The screams were Altur's, each syllable saturated with raw panic. In seconds, I was running to the house, fearing the worst. It was hard to find my way in the moonless night, Altur did his watch in the dark, no fire or lit candles. This had been his home for decades, he would have known the exact location of everything even if he were blind.

"STOP! You can't take her!" His scream came from far behind the house, towards the tree line. I changed course and sped up. Walking countless worlds lends itself to a few tricks and I could move very fast indeed when the situation called for it and I was certain I wouldn't be seen.

I closed on Altur, who was already crashing through the trees, close on the heels of someone else who was making just as much noise. At times, I could hear Edana scream, but it was muffled, like she was gagged.

I didn't let Altur know I was there and pushed my way forward a bit, trying to get a look at Edana's kidnapper. It was too dark to see anything, but I could hear him muttering under his breath as he jogged through the trees.

The man was tireless, even with a struggling woman on his shoulder, but Altur was fueled by powerful emotions and gained steadily.

What happened next took everybody by surprise. Hearing

that Altur wasn't giving up pursuit, the man cast a hand backward and a ball of flame burst out behind him. It rolled over itself as it slammed through the trees to where Altur was pounding his way through the vegetation in his crashing pursuit.

In the light of the fireball, everything was illuminated for a moment. The face of the kidnapper I already knew, it was the man I had seen out on the plains, the one who had killed the other sorcerer.

Edana was trussed up in a bag over his shoulder. The shock of it brought me to a halt. In the same moment, he saw me. And if I was surprised, he was astonished, freezing in his tracks in wonder at seeing me appear out of nowhere not five feet from where he stood.

If his surprise at seeing me wasn't enough, Altur had one more shock in store for him. When the flame ball came rolling at him, he didn't even break stride. In the light of the fire, he saw Edana bouncing around on the man's shoulder. Nothing else mattered.

He barreled right through the wall of flame like a raging bull and came out the other side snorting and bellowing like one as well. The sorcerer's eyes jerked back to him just in time to see the angry man, little flames still alight in his hair, right before he was taken down in a full body tackle.

Altur ducked a shoulder and hit him right in the midriff without breaking stride. The fire thrower folded in half like a piece of paper, knocked out of the air with a stick.

Edana fell off to the side and squirmed wildly in her sack. Altur sat astride the intruder, raining blows down on his face and body, his own chest heaving like a bellows from his sprint through the woods.

The man under him blocked everything he could, but it wasn't much as Altur was in his rage. Where the sorcerer's hands failed, his voice saved him. He said the one thing that could stop Altur mid-swing.

"I can help her!"

Chapter 4

People never know what they are capable of until all other options run out.

–Musings of the Historian

Another ball of flame wouldn't have worked on Altur, but those words hit him like an axe. His fists paused midair and he stared down at the strange man in wonder.

"Can I get up, please?"

He struggled to extricate himself, but the stout farmer held him fast on the ground.

"What do you mean you can help her?"

"Are you some kind of idiot? Do you need me to teach you the words, sonny? She's a raging freak intent on suicide, am I right?"

The stinging words cut at Altur and he nodded silently, not trusting his voice.

"Then even a dumb piece of plodding meat like yourself should know what I'm talking about. Let me up, and let me leave and I will do what I can to stop the madness from destroying her."

"How?"

"Bloody mother of simpletons and farm trash!" The sorcerer thrashed and cursed at Altur, who remained sitting on top of the other man. "Am I the only one who saw me throw fire out of my hands? I have magic, you slab of blubbering beef!

"I'm going to use my shiny, sparkly magic to help your woman's addled freak mind! Do I need to set up a puppet show for you?"

Altur turned his head to where his wife rolled on the ground a few feet away, her screeching an appropriate background for the sorcerer's stream of insults and curses.

"I'm coming with you." Altur's tone left no room for argument. The sorcerer argued anyway.

"I will burn your flesh if you try to follow me again! My mercy is running a little thin. It wasn't much to begin with and now it's suffocating under the weight of your pork-fed carcass. You won't see her again, but you have my word that she'll live a lot longer with me than with you."

"Not good enough." Altur reached a hand down and clamped it on the smaller man's throat. With a tiny flexing of his fingers, the sorcerer was choking and gasping. "Wherever she goes, I go, or you die here. I want your word."

He relaxed his fingers for a second to let his victim breathe. The sorcerer took the opportunity to spit at him and threaten another burning. His threats were cut short as the farmer's fingers tightened again.

"You can burn me all you want, but you can't burn me faster than I can snap your neck. You shouldn't doubt my resolve."

The fingers tightened and lips started turning blue. The sorcerer nodded weakly. Altur released his grip on the other man's neck.

"I have your word?"

"You have my word and you can choke on it, you filth. Tag along if you wish, carry your batty wife while you're at it. All I ask is that you reach inside that sickly little excuse of a brain you've got and rip out whatever hope you still have for a happy ending. This isn't going to end well for you, me, or her. Only death awaits us."

"That's always been true." Altur shrugged and climbed to his feet. He lifted his thrashing wife tenderly, carrying her in his arms like one would hold a sickly child. The sorcerer staggered back to his feet, cursing and spitting. His vile turned abruptly on me.

"Did you get all that, Historian? Did you file away every little comment and nuance? Did the scene strike some chord in your un-beating heart? Well come along, I wouldn't want you to miss anything, you soul sucking parasite."

"W-what?" Like the first time, I found myself completely at a loss as to how to respond to this violent little man who spewed venom with every word and seemed to know things about me that I could only hope weren't true.

"W-w-w-what?" He mocked my voice, stuttering sarcastically. "I'll make you a deal right now, Historian. I suspect that there is a lot you want to ask of me. Oh, yes, I know all about you. And I will drop everything else in this world and answer every question you have if you can answer just one of mine."

"What would you like to know? I'll tell you anything." My breath caught in my throat, the hopes of millennia suddenly laid out before me for trade.

"Your name."

The bottom dropped out from under me. He truly knew what I was, knew it well enough to trap me. He leaned forward dramatically, turning his head to present me with a listening ear.

"Well?"

"His name is Tory." Altur supplied the name helpfully. The sorcerer laughed at the name, guessing its origin at once.

"Is it now? That should solve everything then, shouldn't it? Here, repeat after me, Historian.

"My..."

"My," I followed along dumbly, even though I knew how it would end.

"Name..."

"Name."

"Is..."

"Is."

"Tory." He finished the sentence and looked at me with a broad, wicked smile. I stared back helplessly. My mouth would not shape the word, my voice wouldn't make the tones, and my mind wouldn't command them to do it.

It was like trying to wrap your arms around your chest and lift yourself into the air. The way things were made it impossible. It wasn't a matter of effort.

"What is going on?" There were too many confusing things happening all at once for Altur. He looked back and forth between the two of us, trying to decipher the point of our little game.

"Nothing, Altur," I conceded. It was obvious that I wouldn't get my answers tonight. Still, I had been known to wait decades to see a story through. I could wait a while longer to find out more about my own. "Let's take care of your wife."

Altur nodded, eager to be on his way. The sorcerer shot me

one more derisive snort and led off through the woods. Altur followed and I was right behind him.

The sorcerer followed a path only he could see through endless miles of forest. Of course, that is merely an optimistic guess. After stumbling through various bushes, I had my doubts that there was any path at all.

Regardless, we soldiered on through the night and the next morning. We had to stop a few times for Altur to rest, though his endurance while carrying his wife was quite amazing; even more so when you consider that she was thrashing more often than not.

At every break, the sorcerer took the opportunity to yell at Altur, calling him lazy and letting out long streams of profanity about his weak arms and soft feet.

At one point, I started to defend Altur when something occurred to me. I had been about to say that I didn't think that the sorcerer could have done any better himself. As I went to say it, I realized that he didn't seem tired at all. I practically shouted the question that leapt into my mind.

"Are you a Historian, sorcerer?"

His eyes burned with anger as he turned them on me, irritated to have his tirade interrupted. He stalked over to me, pulled my ear down to his mouth and whispered.

"Wouldn't that be nice? Wouldn't you love to have found a kindred spirit, someone to while away the endless time with? Perhaps we could go for a walk together. There's just one problem, Historian...

"MY NAME IS AEGON!"

He yelled this last part in my ear as loud as he could and my head rang with the volume of it. He turned back to insulting Altur, but try as he might, he couldn't quite get the rhythm of it again and he settled for striking the farmer on the back of the head and sitting down in the dirt to sulk until we were ready to move again.

The day stretched on into the afternoon before we finally reached our destination. It was a ramshackle hut, tucked back into a canyon.

Towering walls of stone rose on both sides, like two massive hands about to clap shut on the tiny dwelling. It was a perfect crude match to Aegon's rough leather clothes, barely patched together. Really not surprising at all.

That made what happened next all the more surprising, though shocking may be a better word for it. As we stepped into the shack, Altur and I froze in our tracks at the horrible sight that lay before us.

The center of the room was dominated by a large, waist-high fire ring with a bellows, the type that might be used by a blacksmith. However, that is where the similarities to a blacksmith shop ended. It's a shame, too, as I've always had a fondness for blacksmiths.

Chains and shackles were bolted to the walls. Hooks, blades, and pincers hung from the ceiling. Charred wood decorated the place, strewn about like black snowflakes. Burn marks also showed on the walls, especially around the shackles. One glance was all it took to deduce the purpose of this twisted little building.

It was a torture chamber.

Chapter 5

No healthy mind could bring itself to torture another human being.
–Musings of the Historian

Altur spun to head back out the door, but Aegon had already blocked the way. The farmer hovered in indecision. To fight his way through, he would have to put his wife down, something he wasn't willing to do yet.

"What is this? What do you mean to do to us?"

"Oh you bleating sheep." Aegon's response was typical of his acidic personality. "What did you expect, clean sheets and soft pillows? The one thing I asked of you was to abandon your hope. I would appreciate it if you would get a start on that.

"Your wife will not be helped with medication or bed rest. I will do as I said, I will help her. But do not imagine that there is any relief, for either of you. If anything, I offer to trade one kind of madness for another."

Altur was about as close to breaking down as that first day I met him. He knew how hopeless his situation was. There was no real chance of her surviving another month. She was already hitting her head on the floor hard enough to draw blood.

"Would she be herself again?" Each word ripped from him

like a sob.

"My, but you are pathetic, farmer. Are we really going to sit here and discuss this? Yes, she will be able to think and speak like other people, but everything changes, I've told you that. She can't go back and play house with you. Not ever.

"Now, you have all of ten seconds to make up your mind. If you don't want my help, take the bag off and there's a lovely river to the east of here where she can drown herself in peace. What's it to be, sheep brain?"

The reference to the river had been too much. Altur broke and handed his wife over to this stranger, though he looked to be struggling under a much heavier weight.

"Please help." The words, almost whispered, were both plea and surrender. Both sentiments were pointless when dealing with some like Aegon, who answered in customary fashion as he turned away, carrying Edana.

"Thank you for making this trip more annoying than usual. I would thank you to leave now, forever, if you think you can handle it."

"I'm not leaving her."

"I guess I saw that coming. Big slab of nothing like you can't think well enough to change its mind, eh? Suit yourself, you can wait outside, but you'll have to figure out your own food. I'm not sharing any of mine."

"I'm not leaving her," Altur repeated, iron in his voice as he set his feet meaningfully.

"Oh for the love of everything sweet and fluffy in this blood forsaken world! What do I have to do to get rid of you? Don't you get it? Didn't the decor give the slightest hint? What is going to happen in this room, you won't want to see. I promise you that on your own mother's life."

"I'm not leaving her."

"LISTEN TO ME!" Spittle sprayed from his lips as he dropped Edana on the ground unceremoniously and stepped over her to scream in Altur's face. "I am going to hurt her! Unless you are some kind of monster, you will try to stop me. I can't have that. GET OUT!"

The fury of his tirade broke like a storm on the firm brow of the simple farmer. Altur didn't move.

"Then bind me. You have the chains for it."

Aegon scratched at his head and tried a different tactic. He changed his tone to be soft and soothing, like one would talk to a child or a pet.

"Look, you seem like a nice little flesh lump; stupid as the day is long, but nice. It would make me so sad to see anything bad happen to you. The environment in here is going to become quite dangerous and you could be hurt. We wouldn't that, would we?"

"I'll risk it."

"Risk what? You don't even know what you're talking about. You may not even survive the experience. I might not survive the experience, and she has less of a chance than either of us. Why would you want to be here for that?"

"I'm not leaving her." The rugged man fell back to his first statement, speaking it like testimony.

"You know what? Great idea! I'm amazed I didn't think of it myself." the sorcerer muttered as he started pacing around the room, picking up wood pieces that weren't completely burned and piling

34

them in the fire pit.

"Best case scenario, you die and I don't have to deal with lump brained farmers any more. No, wait... best case scenario, I die and I don't have to endure any of these fools ever again. There's a winner..."

His mumbling continued as he worked at building his fire. With the matter seemingly settled, Altur dug in to help. He stepped outside and gathered more wood we had seen on our way up. Returning, he laid it by the fire pit where Aegon already had a small fire crackling.

As a thank you, Aegon spat at him, gathered up the armful of wood and piled all of it on the fire. The small flames struggled a bit under the weight of it, but then ate the dry wood hungrily.

The shack was already uncomfortably warm and was getting warmer by the minute. Aegon ordered the farmer out for more wood, instructing him to bring in five more armfuls and put them on the fire.

Altur followed his directions exactly, hurrying around outside the shack, fetching bundle after bundle of wood. As each stack was added to the fire, it grew and writhed in its pit. The hole in the top of the shack wasn't large enough to handle all the smoke and a haze started to fill in around the ceiling.

The big man coughed as smoke filled his lungs as he fought the heat, struggling to get close enough to throw the last armful of wood onto the raging bonfire.

Aegon didn't seem to be bothered by the heat as he arranged black iron pokers and steel blades on the edge of the fire ring, the points stuck in the flames and coals. When things were set up to his satisfaction, he turned to the farmer.

"You first," he commanded, pointing to a wall and the shackles on it. Altur submitted calmly, walking over and locking the iron braces around his ankles. Aegon then helped fasten heavy metal bindings on his wrists, chaining them above his head.

When the farmer was fully secured, he turned to the woman on the floor. She had calmed slightly, possibly overwhelmed by the heat in the room.

He pulled the bag off of her head and dragged her to her feet. She started thrashing to get away from him and he struck her across the face with the back of his hand.

Altur's chains rattled as he instinctively jerked in response. Still, he didn't speak or try to break free. He had thrown all his eggs into this basket, and he would stay on through whatever came.

Aegon wrestled Edana over to another wall, the one closest to the fire. With great difficulty, he managed to clamp the irons onto her wrists and secure them.

Unlike Altur, Edana's hands were fastened right in front of her, though they still chained to the wall on either side. He bent to chain her legs and got a kick to the face for his troubles. Spitting and cursing, he finally managed to get her manacled.

When she was finally secured, he hit her again across the mouth. The look on Altur's face held hatred and murder for the sorcerer, but still he didn't object, keeping his word not to interfere in any way. When Aegon turned to his metal implements in the fire, however, one question popped loose.

"What about Tory? Don't you need to bind him as well?"

"He won't do anything."

"How do you know that?" Altur fixated on this one point, possibly to delay what was coming for Edana. "Why were you so concerned about me getting hurt or stopping you, but you don't seem to care that he is standing right there?"

Altur was right, I stood only an arm's length away. If I had truly been part of the story, there was a lot I could have done to stop him; but both Aegon and I knew that I wouldn't. The hard part was how to explain that to Altur, the farmer.

It wasn't difficult for Aegon, however.

"There's something you should know about your friend."

With that, he snatched a knife from the fire. I only had time to notice the tip glowing a bright red with heat before he plunged it into my chest.

"No!" Altur sprang against his chains, the wood on the walls creaking and straining to hold his weight. The look on Aegon's face was pure delight as he stared into my eyes. He was daring me to give up, to walk away from the story.

It was what usually happened when my secret was revealed. It was too much for people to handle, and every event, every story was tainted by it. There was too much, though, in this story. The mystery was too deep. I couldn't bring myself to leave.

So I stood, motionless, until he pulled the knife out, the tip cooled. No blood stained the knife.

Confusion, bordering on panic, contorted Altur's face as he looked from one of us to the other, not sure anymore who he should fear or what questions to ask.

"Tory?" It was a whimper of a question. He looked at me pleadingly, hoping that I would volunteer some sort of information that would let his world make sense again.

It was a plea that was reflected in my own heart. It was what made it impossible for me to leave. I had the same question Altur did, though I couldn't have put it into words any better than he had.

"I am a witness here, Altur." It wasn't much of an answer for the farmer, but it was all I could offer. "I can't die, as you've seen, but I have no power to help you. I will stay with you until the story is done, if you will allow it."

He nodded dumbly. He didn't understand, but we were beyond grasping at straws. I suspect by now he doubted his own sanity. I couldn't blame him.

Twenty-four hours ago, he had been settling down to keep vigil on his mad wife, awash in tragedy. Now he found himself chained to a wall, about to watch his love be tortured with fire in the company of a sorcerer and a helpless immortal. It was enough to break even a healthy mind.

All he clung to now was that I was the only friendly face in the room. Sanity would have to wait.

When he saw the situation resolved, Aegon grew even more moody. My presence burned at his mind like vinegar on an open wound. He couldn't get rid of me, he knew that, and it made it that much worse.

So it was with a foul temper that he turned to his grisly task. He put the knife back in the fire to heat it up again and pulled a poker out instead. There was no more ceremony or build up.

He grabbed Edana's hand and shoved the bright end of the poker into the flesh of the palm. Her scream was inhuman. I struggle to describe it, though the memory of the sound of it has never left me.

I know well the sounds of pain. I have seen endless tortures and maimings. I have heard the cries of the wounded and broken. Edana's scream was different from anything else I had heard before or anything I've heard since.

There was the wrenching cry of pain, of course, the kind that tears at the throat; but there was more. Laced in with the agony was a tone of exultation. It was the sound of violent victory.

I couldn't help but feel fear as I heard it. It was the sound of purest madness, agony and sadistic joy woven together by a broken mind. It struck a primal chord within me. It was unnatural. Later, I wondered if people sometimes got that feeling when they looked deep in my eyes.

Even Aegon seemed surprised by the intensity of it and he turned an eye to Altur, who had shut his eyes against the horror of the scene. It was a shame that he did, though, for the sorcerer's eyes held a rare glimmer of grudging respect.

"I don't know that I've ever had one this far along before. How in the world did you keep her alive for so long?"

Altur shuddered, keeping his eyes closed. He was trying in vain to filter out some part of what was going on. In my opinion, he was doing it all wrong. Closing your eyes only makes sounds that much more vivid, and the sound was far worse than anything he could see.

Not getting a response from the big farmer, Aegon shrugged and turned back to his task. He replaced his used poker and fetched another glowing one from the fire. This one went to her other hand.

Repetition did nothing to dull the effect of the scream on my soul. If anything, the normal pained cry was being crowded out by the swelling sound of unnatural madness. I actually felt dizzy.

This routine was completed over and over, moving hand to hand, working his way through the various implements he had gathered. Her cries changed with each one.

By the last one, there was no trace of pain. There was only screeching, full of insane joy. He didn't even have to burn her anymore. The cries started before the glowing metal touched her skin. The sound was like a high pitched laugh that didn't stutter or break as a laugh should.

This was what Aegon had been waiting for. Casting the poker to the side, he grabbed both of her hands in his own and then there was flame streaming from his hands, snaking around her arms in red tendrils. Her skin took on a dull red glow, as if the fire was coursing under her skin as well, filling her body.

Now her scream was pure pain, a shriek of agony as fire washed her body, inside and out. The glow grew brighter in Edana's body, as if the flames had filled her.

The next scream came from Aegon.

The key part, I realize now, looking back on it, was that the fire was no longer coming from the sorcerer. The flames that had spouted from his hands were gone now. He no longer gripped her hands. She gripped his and his gnarled fingers looked like they were being crushed by her small, feminine ones.

Though the flames had stopped coming from him, they still filled her and danced over her skin. With another shriek, this one of anger, the flames grew outward, then shot into the sorcerer.

The wall of heat hit him like a fist and knocked him free.

Aegon crumbled to the ground, steam rising off his skin and rough leathers.

Still the flames grew around Edana, vibrating and pulsing outward like a fiery throbbing heart. I looked over to Altur, but his face was turned away as far as he could turn. It looked like he was trying to press his whole body into the wall behind him.

As the flames lit up the room, I could see why; the heat emanating from his wife was burning him. His skin looked like someone who had fallen asleep for hours under a summer sun,; red and raw.

I stood in awe and wonder as the flames danced and throbbed through the chained woman. She yelled and thrashed, but if she was in any pain, it was overshadowed by whatever mad impulse drove the flames.

Finally, it was over. I could not tell you how long it went on, I tend to get caught up in moments like those. Edana hung limp from the chains that held her to the wall.

Altur was also hanging in his chains, though whether dead or unconscious, I couldn't tell. Aegon still lay like a lump on the floor, fresh char marks dotting his clothing and searing into his skin.

So I was left alone for a moment to reflect on what had happened. I had seen Aegon pump his magical fire right into the tortured woman. When it came back out, however, it was far more than he had put in.

In fact, even in his great battle out in the wilderness, I had never seen him conjure anything as powerful as the burning maelstrom Edana had produced.

My mind vibrated with questions, but there was no one to

answer them. All that seemed clear was that Edana was now in command of powerful magic. Command, of course, is likely a bad word for it, as she was totally out of control.

Chapter 6

Curiosity is the hunger of the mind.
–Musings of the Historian

Aegon rose first. He rolled back and forth on the dirt floor of the shack, groaning and cringing as each new burn mark came in contact with the ground. At last, he managed to struggle his way to his knees, opening bloodshot eyes to stare at me.

"Don't suppose you felt any of that, did you, Historian?" I'm sure he meant it as a taunt, but his voice was so tired and raw that it came across as almost sympathetic.

"I could feel the heat, but it couldn't touch me."

He nodded, small tendrils of smoke still rising from his singed hair.

"That's about the way of it. That's how I knew what you were, you know."

"What do you mean, how did you know I was a Historian?" I was a little overeager in my questioning, but this was the closest the two of us had come to a conversation. If being burned, beaten, and kneeling in the dirt was what it took for him to talk, I wasn't about to waste the opportunity fate had handed me.

"You shimmer." He chuckled to himself at his clever reply until a fit of coughing drove him back down to the ground on his hands and knees.

"Shimmer? You mean I'm shiny? Do I glow?" I pressed. His dazed state was fading, and his regular disdain was starting to seep back into his expression.

"No, you don't glow, you deathless block. That might be the stupidest thing I've heard today, and that's quite an accomplishment, considering the company I'm keeping lately."

"Then what did you mean?" I pleaded. The window of opportunity was closing as he recovered from the experience. Some distant corner of my mind considered what it would take to beat and burn him again so that he would talk. He glared at me again through squinted eyes before finally shrugging.

"You aren't all here. It's like seeing a reflection in a still pond, but more. You can walk and talk, touch and be touched, but there is a part of you that isn't really here. You're like a reflection of another reality, like the reflection in the pond is the real thing and you are the imaginary part walking around on the land side. So, you shimmer."

"You can see that?" I whispered in awe. There was nothing I had ever seen and no one I had ever met that had made me doubt the nature of my own existence. But here in a burned shack with unconscious people hanging from the walls, this kneeling sorcerer explained things I could never have imagined like they were simple truths.

"No, of course I can't see this, you stupid, whiny, piece of shimmering garbage." Aegon was fully recovered now, struggling to his feet. He spewed more venom than usual, probably a side effect of being in a lot of pain and revealing more to me than he had intended.

"Then how do you know?" I knew it was over, he was back to his old self, and angry at me for taking advantage of him in his weakened state. Still, I had to try. Surprisingly, I got lucky and he gave me one last gem.

"My fire. It is a part of me and I can feel with it, see with it, it is a part of me and a part of everything around me. I can sense reality through it. But my fire can't touch you.

"It's not that it runs up against you and can't harm you. It runs right through the space where my eyes tell me you are, but the fire tells me that there is nothing there. This combination of senses fight with each other. My eyes tell me there's a man in front of me, my magic assures me there is not.

"Like I said, you shimmer, and the only thing I'm sure of by eyes, ears, and magic, is that you don't have a brain, since I need to spoon feed you every scrap of knowledge you keep panting after like a starved dog."

He was opening his mouth to start another insult when he was interrupted by a groan from the wall behind us. The smoke and heat had cleared enough and Altur was waking up. Aegon went over and took the chains off of his hands. Unfortunately, he was still a little dizzy and fell over, the chains on his feet keeping him from catching himself.

He landed with a thud and groaned loudly from the dirt floor. I went over to help him get the chains off his feet. As soon as he was back standing, we all circled around Edana. She hung limply from the bindings on the wall. In spite of her awkward position, her breathing was smooth and deep, like a sleeping child.

There were marks on her hands, but nothing like there should have been. I had expected nothing less than charred flesh from the combination of red hot metal, Aegon's magic, and her own fiery combustion.

There were burn marks on her hands where the pokers had been set against her skin, but they were superficial, like what someone might get putting their hand on a hot stove. Her arms were completely clean, in spite of the ribbons of flame I had seen running over them like writhing snakes.

"Why isn't she burned?" I asked Aegon. A derisive snort was his only response, his time of answering questions was over.

"When will she wake up?" It was Altur's turn to question the sorcerer. All he got for his trouble was a shrug.

There was nothing else to be said or done. Under different circumstances, I imagine Altur would have been asking a million questions of me. As it was, he was completely focused on his wife. The traumatic scene he had endured, watching his wife be tortured and then burst into flame from the inside out was probably more than his mind could process.

For his simple, uneducated mind, it was enough that his wife was still alive and right in front of him. Questions could wait, forever if need be.

"Thank you for helping her."

This humble offering of gratitude from the farmer was enough to rouse Aegon from his own reverie.

"What is wrong with you?" he snapped at the farmer. Altur stuttered, trying to find a response for the sudden attack. Aegon didn't give him a chance to get his balance, but pressed his verbal attack.

"I am having a truly hard time figuring out what defect you

could have been born with. Or perhaps this is the effect of too many hours out under the sun rooting around in the dirt. I only asked you one thing, just one thing. How bloody hard is it, even for a dumb farmer to remember one thing? Now what did I ask you to do?"

Aegon's screaming face was inches from Altur's as his tirade reached its peak.

"To give up hope," the farmer whispered. Aegon reached up and patted the larger man's head, like one would do to a child.

"My, my, already you surpass my expectations, farmer. What a bright little boy you are. Now tell me, if your brain managed all of that, why can't you do it?"

"I'm just grateful that you tried to help, you gave us a chance." Altur's defense was humble and sincere, but it only served to escalate the sorcerer into a spitting rage.

"Chance?" He screamed the word. "There is no chance! There is no bloody chance! There is not on this cold grave of a rock a single bloody, soul-sucking chance! Bend your dirt-filled ears forward like one of your dumb cows and listen to me! We are all dead.

"I have saved your wife from death by river so that she might die a much worse one. Care to know what happens to me? If I'm very lucky, I get to die first. I swear to you, by the hide and hair of every mother who was ever disappointed by a stupid farmer son, that what I am telling you is true.

"The only mystery left to me is how any man, even a dirt bred farmer like yourself, can somehow not exercise enough sense to get as far away from this as possible. Any beast in any field knows to run from fire. Why not you?"

"I love her." The sorcerer rolled his eyes at Altur's simple sentiment.

"Great, love her from far away. Treasure up your warm memories with her, they'll comfort you when winter comes. There are no new warm memories coming, not down this road. You'd do best to leave and keep hold of your life and your memories."

"I'm not leaving her, I don't care what comes."

"You might, by the end of this." The anger had played out, and Aegon's voice was calm again. He dismissed the farmer from his mind with a wave of his hand and turned back to his chained charge.

It wasn't long before she began to stir. Aegon leaned forward and shook her roughly. He eyes lolled open for just a moment, then closed again. The sorcerer grunted his impatience and took to patting her on the cheek. It wasn't gentle, but it wasn't really a slap, either.

The eyes opened again and glared irritation at the sorcerer. As comprehension dawned, however, fear crept into her eyes. She tried to reach her hand to her face, but it was still chained. Her breath quickened as panic set in. She shot another pleading look at Aegon, desperately searching for answers or help.

Not seeing anything helpful in Aegon's face, she looked to me, but didn't seem to recognize me, though I had been around her for most of a month. It was then that her eyes swung to Altur and held there. She peered for a second, trying to make out his features in the dim lighting. Finally, recognition lit her eyes and she spoke.

"Altur, what am I doing here?"

Chapter 7

True love yearns to have love returned to it, but it can do without in a pinch.

–Musings of the Historian

It is said that about three quarters of communication is nonverbal, which leaves only a quarter in the words themselves. Everything else is in the tone, the inflection, and the body language of the person speaking.

In my experience, three quarters seems like an awfully low estimate. Words are weak communicators, and easily misunderstood. The nonverbal cues, however, tone and body language, communicate on a level words never could. Nonverbal communication can weave attitude, emotions, and any number of other subtleties into fractions of a second.

The true limitation of writing stories down is that these rich flavors of communication are lost. Normally, it doesn't matter enough to bring it up, the words do enough to relate how people are feeling and the listener's imagination fills in the blanks.

In this case, however, the words Edana spoke to Altur were but a ragged sliver of what was communicated in that moment. Her tone, her inflections, and what body language was possible while chained to a wall all screamed one thing:

Altur was her servant.

The revelation was all the more shocking to me because I had been so completely converted by Altur's absolute love. I had fallen into the trap of assumptions.

I had assumed that Edana would look at her husband with love, or at least hope and gratitude at seeing a familiar face. Instead, her voice commanded a response and expected to be obeyed. A subtle contempt ran through her voice. It was obvious that she considered Altur to be beneath her.

It occurred to me that perhaps the madness and magic had somehow twisted her mind. After all, it wasn't hard to believe with Aegon standing right next to me, ready with insults and tirades for one and all. Maybe this magic pushed people into contempt for all around them.

I turned to study Altur's face. It would have been impossible for him to miss the way she had just spoken to him. If it was a new thing, caused by the magic, then he would be hurt and shocked by the transformation.

He was neither.

In fact, his head bobbed when she spoke to him, an unconscious bow before his mistress. She had expected to be obeyed because he was used to obeying her. This large farmer who had charged through fire and stood up to a sorcerer now fidgeted and hastened to explain.

"You were taken by the madness. This man said he could help you. The chains are there so you wouldn't hurt yourself. We can take them off now, right?"

"No." Aegon's voice was dark.

Edana's eyes flashed with anger and she turned on the

sorcerer who had denied her freedom. The anger flickered and died when it crashed against Aegon, however. She was fully in her element bossing her husband around, but when she met the hard eyes of the sorcerer, her resolve crumbled and she was suddenly just a woman chained to a wall.

"Please let me go," she whimpered, submitting to Aegon as completely as Altur had submitted to her only seconds before.

"No," he repeated. "We have some things to talk about first."

"All right."

"You have magic now," he started out directly, never one for small talk that didn't include yelling. "And I need your help, I will need you to use your magic to fight."

It was too much. Months of madness, punctuated by torture and magic, waking up to chains and bizarre demands for violence broke her down. Racking sobs shook her body as pent up emotions flowed free in a steady stream of tears. Aegon groaned loudly and rubbed at his temples.

"I remember why I prefer my own company," the sorcerer complained. "I should have chosen a life of solitude, however short it might be, before I let myself be caught amongst fools, hysterical women, and psychopaths."

It took me a moment to comprehend that the psychopath comment was directed at me, though I couldn't even begin to imagine what he might be referring to. Still, it disturbed me.

Altur tried to comfort her. In a way, it worked. She didn't take any comfort from his words, but being reminded of his presence provided an anchor to the familiar.

She was ashamed to be crying in front of him. I could hope it was out of respect for his opinion, but it was all too obvious that it was the kind of shame one feels showing weakness in front of a servant. With lots of sniffing, she pulled herself together and addressed Aegon again, focusing on one impossibility at a time.

"What do you mean I have magic? What kind of magic could I have?"

"There's only one kind of magic, woman." The sorcerer obviously did not enjoy his role of school teacher, but he plowed into his explanation. Altur and I were glued to the scene as the irritating man finally parted with some answers, however grudgingly.

"The madness that takes people isn't truly madness, it's magic. It builds up inside of your head, but it doesn't have any place to go. It's an emotion that slowly builds, like water filling a lake until it starts to flow over the dam."

"An emotion? What kind of emotion?" I asked. Aegon glared daggers at me for interrupting, but he answered.

"You don't have the emotion, so I can't explain it to you. It would be like trying to explain colors to a blind man. As near as I can tell, it's like a happy rage. The point is, it builds up inside a person. It's like when someone buries sadness in their heart. It grows until it consumes them or they break and let it all out. Anyone who has been in that situation knows what a full body experience that is.

"This magic works much the same way. It's like an itch in your mind, nothing you've felt before and nothing you could name or recognize, but it's there all the same. It grows and grows, demanding more of your mental resources. It will consume a mind entirely unless there is a release."

"The fire?" Altur prompted. He received another

condescending pat on the head.

"Yes, my dumb farmer, the fire. Whether the emotion is the magic itself, or they're connected in some other way, the emotion dies down as the fire rages."

"What fire?" Panic was creeping back into Edana's voice.

"This fire." Aegon lifted a hand and produced a small fire ball that curled around itself, rising up to the roof and dissipating with a flash. Edana's chin quivered again and it looked like she might become hysterical again.

"So I can do that?"

"No, stupid girl, you can't. All you can do right now is burst into flame and torch everything around you. You haven't developed your power yet. You haven't learned to recognize and channel the emotion yet. All you can do is release it. Right now, you can't even do that, the reservoir inside your mind is bone dry."

"Oh," she whispered, not sure whether she should be comforted or not. "So I need to learn how to use it? How do I do that?"

For the first time, a flash of genuine pity flashed across Aegon's face, but it was gone so fast I wonder even now if I truly saw it.

"You will have to use your magic. At the moment of release, you will come into direct contact with the emotion. Your mind will rebel against it, you will struggle to grasp it, but you will get threads of the thing, enough to give it direction. It's an all or nothing sort of thing. Once you break the dam inside your mind, the magic will flow out of you in a fury, you won't be able slow or stop it until it is all gone, as it is now."

"But you don't do that." Altur made the observation. "You use as much magic as you need, no more."

"Shut your mouth, filth." Aegon spat the words at the farmer. Even being used to the sorcerer's abrasive nature, we were still dumbfounded by the passion in his words. "You don't know what you're talking about."

"I'm sorry," Altur stammered, reeling from the unexpected attack.

"You are sorry, a sorry piece of nothing that has caused me nothing but trouble."

"Hey now!" Edana scolded. "There's no call for that!"

Aegon groaned again, even louder.

"You children have no idea what is called for or not. Nevertheless, you would have to find out eventually what we're up against.

"The fact is that we have an enemy. It is an enemy of my own making and the war we fight cannot be won, but it must be fought."

Weariness lay heavy in his words. I reflected on what he had said earlier about sadness consuming a person when it was locked away inside. As near as I could tell, Aegon had sadness and much more locked away inside himself, so much that the bitterness of it was overflowing.

"Who is this enemy?" I asked. It was a sign of Aegon's true sorrow and weariness that he didn't even take the time to level an insult at me before answering.

"My students."

Chapter 8

Teachers see coldness in the world and light fires in the minds of their students, hoping for a warm summer. Sadly, some cannot bear the flame, some turn away from the heat, and some twist the fire to burn.

–Musings of the Historian

"I was the first to master the madness, to unlock the magic. After a while and some devastating failures, I discovered how to unlock it in others, to free them from their madness.

"Most of them stayed with me and we studied together, refining the magic as best we could. Some few only learned enough to safely release it and then went back to their lives. We will need to seek some of them out before this is all over.

"The beginning of the end focused around a boy named Humeer, barely twenty when he first joined us. He worked harder than the others to develop his skills, but he was frustrated by the slowness of it. He noticed that I could do more than everyone else. I could stop the flow, for instance, save some magic within myself rather than letting it all out at a go.

"There was a great amount of discussion on the subject, everyone had their own theory. The opinion everyone finally settled on was that I could do more because I had unlocked the power myself, without help; everyone but Humeer.

"He couldn't accept the simple answer because it left him no way to gain it for himself. He kept looking deeper and deeper into the nature of the magic. It was he who first described it as an emotion. He had a brilliant mind and kept delving deeper and deeper to understand how it worked.

"I had unlocked the magic, but it was Humeer who truly learned to understand it, and soon he was more teacher than I was. I think it was inevitable that he was the one who figured it out. He had figured it out long before any of us knew it. Suddenly he began to progress much faster than anyone else. Within a month he was fully my equal, if not my better.

"To his credit, he came to me first with his discovery. He could have easily taken the school over, or gone directly to the students with the secret of his new power. I think there was a part of him left over that wanted to be vindicated. He wanted my approval, my praise even."

"What was the discovery?" Edana had been listening intently and asked the question burning most in her mind. Whatever Humeer had discovered, it was somehow tied to why she was chained to a wall. Her impatience was understandable.

"The emotion that drove the magic was far too dim, too foreign to nature for the mind to process, so direct control was exceedingly difficult. All the other emotions that run rampant in our heads cause far too much interference. It's like trying to listen to a whisper in a room where everyone is yelling."

A sick feeling had started welling in my stomach. I had an idea where this was going and I really didn't like it. His next statement confirmed my fears.

56

"The natural emotions had to be pushed down, destroyed if possible."

As if sensing my understanding, he turned his head and locked eyes with me. True sadness passed between the two of us in that moment. We both knew what it took to destroy natural emotions, and what it meant for the person who did it. Altur and Edana did not, however, and they interrupted one another to ask the question.

"How can you destroy an emotion?"

"Murder." Edana gasped at Aegon's reply and Altur looked a little pale. The sorcerer's somber tone took on a little more of his regular attitude as he started to distance himself from the subject. "Cruelty, torture, any manner of unspeakable things. Pretty much anything that makes you so sick you want to die.

"Humans are social creatures, herd animals, really. We are tied to each other by bonds we don't really understand, but we need each other. Every part of the mind rebels at deadly violence against another person. The brain simply can't handle it, so it distances itself. It deadens the natural emotions and pushes man's nature closer to that of a machine."

"It's something you see all too often in murderers or soldiers who have been too long at war," I chipped in. "Their humanity leaves them, their ability to feel happiness, sadness, even anger declines. It is like their soul shrivels away inside them and they are left with an emptiness inside."

"And in this emptiness," Aegon continued my thought seamlessly. "The emotion that controls the magic becomes prominent, and it can be felt more directly. It can be controlled, pulsed, moderated, and twisted."

"So your talent with the magic is because..." Altur couldn't quite bring himself to finish his question. Aegon sneered at him.

"Yes, I've killed people. I told you already that there were failures when I tried to unlock the magic in others. People died, horribly, at my hands. You were here, you bloody moron, and surely even a head as thick as yours can imagine what it might be like if it went wrong."

Altur shuddered a bit at the thought. It would be the stuff of nightmares, the work of demons.

"I kept going because I told myself it would all be worth it if I could save people from the madness. But rationalizations do nothing at all to spare your soul from the effects of what you've done. You can tell yourself all you want that the ends justify the means, but it won't erase the screams from your memory. It won't stop your mind from hardening in reaction to the horror.

"By the time I had my first success, I already had more control over my magic than many of them would ever realize. I didn't know the reason for it, I had assumed it was the natural improvement that comes of long practice."

"What happened to your students?" Edana's sudden question hit on the heart of the matter. One didn't have to think very hard to see that Aegon's little narrative was going to end in tragedy. For someone hanging in chains as the newest student, no question could have been more pressing.

"I condemned Humeer for what he had done, preaching to him on the evils of the path he had chosen. Then I did something much worse. I took his case to the students. Up to that point in time, there had been no crime in our little society. Now we were faced with dealing with a murderer. I should have taken the responsibility myself, but I was a fool.

"The students decided on banishment. It wasn't much of a punishment for his crimes, but he had been a teacher among them. There wasn't a single person among them whom Humeer hadn't helped. They couldn't bring themselves to administer the punishment that was likely deserved.

"Then tragedy struck. He left, but people followed. It was in that moment that I realized what a huge mistake I had made."

"How many left?"

"I had just under fifty students at the time, fourteen followed after Humeer. It was devastating to everyone who stayed behind. Loyalties were stretched beyond their breaking point, watching friends walk away.

"Sitting and watching them leave was my next fatal mistake. I knew, even then, that the only reason that they would follow him would be to learn his methods. Bearing that knowledge, I should have attacked and killed them all right then, when I still had the power to do so."

"How could you have killed your own students?" Altur offered the question as comfort, suggesting that Aegon wasn't the kind of monster who could turn on those he loved so easily. It was an easy excuse. Like most of Altur's comments, it only served to enrage the sorcerer.

"If I live as long as a Historian, I will still not comprehend the magnitude of your idiocy, farmer. It stuns me that your farm has managed to exist as long as it has. Let's see if I can't get this down to a level you'd understand. Say your dog got in a fight with a wild dog and came home sick and frothing around the mouth. What would you do?"

"I'd put him down," Altur admitted.

"Oh no you wouldn't!" Aegon crowed. "That would suggest some smattering of common sense, which you obviously lack. No, you would pet and fawn over the creature, feeding it choice pieces of meat, hoping it would get better. You would blubber about how much you loved it. I would further predict an excess of tears and snot.

"I wonder if you would even raise your hand against the beast when it started ravaging your stock, tearing the throats from sheep right and left just for the joy of it. I suspect you would sit and cry over the sheep as well until the dog finally turned on you and put you out of your misery."

Altur knew enough not to respond at all. We had known Aegon less than a day, but we had learned that there were no shortcuts through his tirades. Saying anything at all would only add fuel to the fire.

"So it lives as my eternal shame that on that day I was as dumb as the dumbest farmer I have ever met. I stood there and watched a rabid dog prance off with fourteen other dogs, all eager for the infection. They returned a year later, almost exactly, this time to attack."

"Why would they attack you? You weren't any threat to them." Edana tried to wrap her mind around the savagery of a student returning to destroy all of his friends. I'm afraid it made all too much sense to me. Aegon explained what was already in my mind.

"You can only destroy your soul so much killing strangers.

Morals and sensitivities must be completely drowned away in sin, and there is no greater sin than betrayal. They came to kill us because it would be hard on them, to butcher the best friends they had known. Such an act would surely go far to root out any remaining pieces of a soul they might have had left after a year of carnage in distant villages.

"Their power had grown more than I ever could have expected. We outnumbered them three to one at that point, and they waded through us like a grizzly bear swatting kittens. I managed to gather a band around me and focused our powers together. Doing so we were able to take down one of the fifteen. It made enough of a break in their attack that we were able to slip through their lines and escape. There were only about ten of us who survived.

"The running battle pushed us far into the wilderness. More of my students died. When we finally managed to get away from them, there were only four of us left. We wandered in the wilds for a little while, living off the land, making sure the others wouldn't find us, though I don't think they were even looking any more.

"We might have managed to rebuild, but an insidious idea had crept into our tiny band of survivors. Humeer had been right. Their power was undeniable. They could wield the fire like it was a living extension of themselves. For one of my students, a man named Turon, it ate away at his mind that the power to save himself was within his reach. It didn't take long for him to act on his dark desires.

"The first couple of deaths seemed accidental. The woman in our group became sick and died in the night, victim of his poison. The next man slipped as we crossed near a steep canyon and lost his life on the rocks below. It was then that I started to suspect. It looked like Turon had been grabbing for him to try and catch him, but looks can be deceiving.

"I hid my suspicion, but too late. He saw that I suspected. The next attack had no subtlety at all. Turon knifed him while he slept, that very night as I still struggled with what I must do. He ran off, leaving me alone. I tracked him through the wilderness for days before I finally caught up with him. His power had grown and he proved fairly formidable, but I succeeded in putting him down."

"That's what I saw, wasn't it? The man you killed in the wilderness was your last student," I interjected.

He nodded.

Chapter 9

Perception is reality. Few realize the true depth of that statement.

–Musings of the Historian

"In the time since, I have crossed the mountains and tracked them back to where they have based their operations. They have claimed for their own a small farming community on the far side of this very mountain. They build their power by visiting atrocities upon the villagers there. The poor wretches who live there believe that they have become subject to cruel gods who demand sacrifice. I can't say they're far wrong."

"You expect me to fight these people? Am I supposed to kill innocent people to enhance my own power?" Edana raved. "You can't ask me to do that, even if I do have magic!"

"Shut up!" Aegon slapped her and then turned on Altur, who had started to protest, staring him down until he backed away. "We have come a long way past a simple matter of right and wrong, you sniveling whelps.

"Those remaining fourteen students come from this land. You might even know some of their families. How long will it be before they decide that greater treachery is needed in their pursuit of power? How long before these rivers steam and flow with blood from the savagery of their magic?

"Your land has been losing a war for a long time. What I offer you is the chance to actually put up a bit of a fight before you are butchered like sheep for the enjoyment of the deranged."

"Please, you can't ask her to do this!" Altur pleaded.

"I can, I do, and it's not asking!" Aegon insisted. "I will have to live with my great mistake for the rest of time, but rest assured I will not repeat it."

Once again, Edana and Altur struggled with confusion, not comprehending the full import of what had happened to Aegon.

"What do you mean?"

"I mean that the knowledge of power by murder is dangerous, possibly the most dangerous weight this world has ever had to bear. That knowledge sat right in front of me, a sprouting weed that should have been crushed under heel. I have condemned this world to fire because I let it escape. And now I have shared that knowledge with you."

Understanding dawned on their faces. They had sat and listened to the sorcerer's tale of woe like children listening to a scary story around the campfire. They had not understood the responsibility it gave them, or the lengths Aegon would go to in order to ensure that the secret did not spread any further.

If they tried to leave, he would kill them. As we sat in that smoky shack and watched the conviction that burned in his eyes, none could doubt it. Edana broke down sobbing again in her chains.

"How do you expect us to fight? You lost to them with magic and strength of numbers! What chance do we have?" Altur had seamlessly included himself in the fight now that he knew his wife had no way out.

"Does it matter?" Aegon raged right back at him, though this time, the farmer stood his ground. "I am going to fight them, or be damned. Your wife is going to fight them, or die here. And you are going to fight them because you were too bloody stupid to leave before and you certainly haven't gotten any smarter."

"What about Tory?" Altur's concern for my well-being was touching, though now even he had to know that my life wasn't truly at stake. Aegon turned and looked at me as if surprised I was still there.

"Him? He will walk away at the end of all this. And one day he will pronounce judgment on us as he tells his stories, all wise and smug as we rot in our graves."

Surprisingly, Altur accepted this in stride. Edana didn't even bat an eyelash. I guess they had reached their limit already, one more flip of reality didn't matter too much anymore.

"I meant, will he fight with us?"

"Yes."

It was a shocking answer. I had never actually fought, at least as far as I could remember, not in earnest. It was ingrained in my very soul that I was an observer, not a participant in these stories. But all of those surprises paled in comparison to the one big surprise:

I was the one who said it.

My surprise paled in comparison to Aegon's, and for the first time, he was at a loss for words.

"What?" His voice echoed my sentiments, but my answer wasn't without reason and I spoke quickly to set my terms.

"If you will tell me what you know, I will do whatever I can to help you win this little war of yours. Deal?"

"What can you do?" The question was sincere. Even though he knew more about me than I knew myself, even he didn't know what rules applied when a Historian broke that barrier and became part of a story.

"I'm not sure," I admitted. It was a first for me as well. "It's not like anything physically restrains me. I just can't make certain decisions at certain times. This will be the first time I try to fight it."

"It's a fascinating idea," he mumbled, more to himself than to any of us. He was staring me down, seeing me for the first time. "I'm pretty sure you can't kill."

"Why not?"

"It just makes sense," he shrugged. "I'm not going to tell you everything now. I will keep up my end as you keep up yours. I won't bet a clod of dirt on the honor of a Historian, and you'd be a fool to trust me. So let's just take it one step at a time."

"That works for me." I held out my hand to seal the deal. In a day made for surprises, he took it and shook it firmly.

A look started to grow in his eyes. It was a most disturbing look. He peered at me like a dog eyeing a bone. He still hadn't let go of my hand from the handshake and he only gripped it harder now. A throaty giggle escaped him and he brought his other hand up, gripping my hand in both of his and shaking with abandon.

"I have it!" he announced. "I have a role for you, my dear Historian. I have a piece of the puzzle that will fit you perfectly."

Everything about it made me feel more uncomfortable than I think I had ever felt. His voice was full of insane eagerness. I was too afraid to ask, but he sat there waiting for it, shaking my hand and grinning at me like an idiot. Edana finally broke the silence.

"What's he going to do?"

"He's going to lead us!" Aegon crowed in response, before falling victim to a fit of high-pitched laughter that threatened to bring him clear to the ground with convulsions. I imagine he would have been literally rolling on the ground, chortling at his own cleverness if he hadn't still been holding onto my hand.

I felt sick. My guess is he knew it. In under two minutes the situation had escalated from me merely participating, to playing a key role.

"Tory's the leader now?" Altur was confused at the turn of events, naturally; but relief was heavy in his voice as it seemed possible that someone, anyone, would be leading the party besides Aegon. The sorcerer nodded his confirmation, as he was laughing too hard to voice his reply. Tears traced down his face as his laughter shook his body.

"Could I ask why?" Edana's question was perfectly valid. I had to say, she was handling the situation surprisingly well for someone chained to a wall. It was a solid minute before Aegon calmed down enough to answer. We all waited.

"Three reasons, my dear. First of all, Tory here can't die." He almost started laughing again when he used my assigned name, but managed to rein it in. "That gives our party the benefit of continuous leadership, won't have to muck about figuring out succession when I finally get what's coming to me.

"Secondly, there is no one living or dead who knows more about human nature than a Historian. The chances of us winning this war are virtually nonexistent, but if somebody can figure out a way around these impossible obstacles, it's him."

Aegon paused in his explanation to give me a low, mocking bow.

"And last of all, I made him leader because everything in his whole being is going to fight him on it, and I love watching him squirm like snake under my boot heel."

It was the happiest I ever saw Aegon. The smile on his face was broad and warm, the kind that comes from a bubbling over of inner joy. Altur and Edana shot me concerned looks. They hadn't understood hardly anything of what Aegon had said, but they caught that it would be bad for me. They were good enough people to pity me, understanding or no. A thought occurred to Edana.

"You can't die?"

I nodded glumly. I felt violated. It was like having all of your most dark secrets posted on a wall for all to see, with illustrations.

"Can we learn your magic?" It hurt me to wipe out the hope she had started to feel.

"No, it's not magic, or at least none that I am aware of. It is simply a fact of my existence. I could no more teach it to you than you could teach me how to grow long hair."

"Your hair is a little long." It was a feeble attempt at a joke, said to break the awkwardness. I decided there was no way of getting around this situation. I had committed myself to this story. I decided to take the next step and divulge some secrets myself. It would be taking control of the situation, in a way.

"Tell me, Edana, what does my hair look like? Be as specific as you can."

A moment of studying followed a moment of confusion, then she offered her description.

"It's just past your ears, brown, about like mine. It curls a bit around the bottom. That's about all I can say, is that good enough?"

"You did great. Now, could you describe the emotion on your husband's face?"

"He looks confused, he's looking at me like I'm crazy."

"Of course he is, but don't mind him. Altur, could you please tell your wife what my hair looks like?"

"Umm, look, I don't want to..." he fumbled, not wanting to contradict his wife.

"Just do it," I pressed.

"It's a light sandy brown, much lighter than hers, and you've got it cropped close. Pretty rough work, too, did you do it with a knife?"

I nodded and turned to Aegon.

"Your turn."

"Black." The sorcerer needed no urging and dug right in. "I see it slicked back from your forehead, like you'd worked some kind of grease into it."

"Thank you, Aegon." He nodded magnanimously and started giggling again. I turned back to my confused farm couple. "You see, I am always a little bit different to each person. I have never had two people describe me in exactly the same way.

"This is not magic, this is something in your world that doesn't belong. Your mind fills in the blanks for you, forcing an image to make me fit into your reality.

"The point I'm trying to make here is that I won't always be able to explain myself. Many things I don't understand, and those few I do understand wouldn't make much sense to you. If I am going to lead this group, I will have to tell you how things have to be and you'll have to accept them on faith. Can you do that?"

"Oh yes!" Aegon exclaimed in mock sincerity. "Can I call you Master?"

"I really wish you wouldn't." I instantly regretted my words. The glee written on his face told me he would call me nothing else from here on out. I ignored him and turned back to the other two.

"I guess I can. I know you're a good man, Tory." Altur's pledge of loyalty produced a new fit of laughter in the sorcerer behind me.

"I guess I don't have much of a choice, do I?" Edana said, clinking her chains symbolically.

"I'm afraid not. From the sound of things, the choice has already been made. War is coming, if you can even call it that. These fourteen are going to come to burn, butcher and enslave. Not knowing how much time we have, we'll have to move as fast as we can to gather all the allies we can get. No one's going home."

Tears were starting down her face again, but she nodded.

"Altur, get those chains off of her," I commanded and he gratefully leapt to obey. I turned to Aegon. "We need more troops. You mentioned others who had learned to control their magic and went back to their lives. We'll need to find them and bring them with us. Can you find them?"

"Yes, Master."

This time I didn't give him the satisfaction of seeing how much the title annoyed me.

Chapter 10

There are some fools out there who believe that a story is a series of events. Events are nothing, even the most terrible or awe-inspiring. A story is made up of the interactions between the people in it.

*   *-Musings of the Historian*

It's hard to describe the feelings with which I struggled. On the one hand, it was actually quite liberating not to maintain a cover story. I no longer had to eat or drink or pretend I was sleeping at night. I was able to be truly honest with people, something I had never been. It made me happy in some place very deep within me.

On the other hand, participating so directly in a story affected me in ways that are hard to describe. Every time I had to make a decision for the group, it was like breaking down a wall in my mind. It was a phenomenon similar to my inability to claim a name, though nowhere near as strong.

The decision itself was usually ridiculously easy. With generations of history at my command, solutions to problems were as clear as daylight. The problem always came when I tried to share my decision with the group. Forming the words was difficult; not impossible, but difficult.

As a result, whenever I gave commands to the group, I spoke

too slowly, stuttered, and slurred my words. If anyone had chanced upon our group, they would have to assume that the party had elected the village idiot to lead them.

Luckily for me, Aegon's impatience made it so I never had to give a command twice. He would even interrupt me once he got the idea of what I was saying and start barking at the other two to carry out what I wanted. I was grateful when he did that, though he made it quite clear that his reasons for doing so had nothing to do with my welfare.

My relationship with the sorcerer was a strange one. He never missed an opportunity to hurl abuse my way and his tongue never lacked for imaginative insults. Still, he jumped to obey my every suggestion, accomplishing most tasks before Altur or Edana could figure out what I meant.

Our camp was mobile. There was no way to know where our enemy was, when they would attack, or how strong they had become. There was no hiding place so secret or fortress so strong that I would trust it with so many unknowns in the balance.

Instead, our strategy was to approach the formless; drifting like the wind, leaving no trail and forming no patterns. From Aegon I learned where we needed to go to find more magic users, but we traveled there in such a way that it was as if we had stumbled upon the places accidentally.

The first one we contacted ended in tragedy. It was a man named Yurt, one of Aegon's earlier pupils. We found him living like a hermit in the hills above a small hamlet. After I explained the whole situation, Yurt started pressing for more information about Humeer and where he might find him. When he could get no more from us, he attacked, hurling a wall of searing hot fire right at my chest.

It was his last mistake.

His pillar of fire absorbed harmlessly into my chest. Aegon's counterstrike was more effective and we left Yurt dead in his hut as it burned down around him. It was a depressing start to our mission.

"He had always been close to Humeer," Aegon pondered aloud. "I suppose I should have suspected that he would side with him. But I couldn't well have passed over him, he was one of my most powerful students."

"We aren't going to win this on power, boy," I scolded him. I had taken to calling him "boy," in a rather juvenile retribution for him calling me master. It was a petty thing, but I just couldn't help myself.

"Oh wise Master," he retaliated, laying the sarcasm on as thick as tree bark. "Please forgive me, your humble servant was being thorough again, I'll try to avoid that in the future, you pad-footed old cheese."

"Your insults don't even make sense any more, you sniveling pup." My communications with Aegon had greatly improved once I figured out that insulting him back made him much more likely to pay attention. "Why don't you be thorough on your own time and take us to someone who might actually join us."

"My insults make perfect sense, you've just spent too much time watching puppet shows, clapping and giggling like a moron."

I thought it a little low of him to attack my stories like that, but he led off, taking us to our next destination. So it was with Aegon, a constant back-talking obedience.

The farm he led us to was a nearly perfect mirror of Altur

and Edana's farm. I guess it was because of the similarities that I assumed that the couple who stepped out to meet us were married. Aegon, of course, had made it a point to leave certain details out. It didn't take me long to embarrass myself.

"Hello, Matt, I was wondering if we might come in and talk to you and your wife."

He might have been thirty, but it was hard to tell. He had the tanned face and worn look of a farmer that made him look older, but the grin that split his face would have been more at home on a six year-old.

"Wahl, dat would be some trick, suh." Matt spoke with an easy drawl, slow and drawn out like he wasn't going to waste the energy it took to form full words. "Ah tell you what, you find me a gurl what's willin' t'marry me and Ah'll let you jaw at us all day, how 'bout?"

"I'm sorry, I assumed when I shouldn't have." I apologized while Aegon sniggered behind me.

"Oh don't you worry none. As soon as Ah saw Aegon wit'ya, I figgered that he figgered that you'd figger we was married, but this is mah sista, Gracie. Ah hope ya don't mind me havin' a smatter of fun at your expense."

"Not at all." Matt had the kind of personality that made people like him instantly. There was a genuineness about him that made you feel like you could trust him with anything, though piecing a meaning together from his convoluted sentences took a second to think through. "And I hope I didn't offend you either, Gracie."

"Of course not. Please come in, it's a hot day and I've got

some cool water inside." Her voice was warm and inviting. Gracie shared absolutely none of her brother's accent, rather each word was clear and refined. As they must have started out the same, it made me wonder which sibling had changed.

They refused to let us talk any business until each of us had been served water and food, even insisting that we take our shoes off to rest our feet. Gracie's insistence stuttered just a moment when she saw my bare feet, but she was too gracious of a hostess to mention it.

She reminded me of a river, the way she flowed around the room, seeing to everyone's comforts without ever being in anyone's way. And if she was a river, her brother was a stone. He situated himself in the center of the room, sprawled out in a chair and chatting to each of us in turn about the weather and what game we'd seen in the hills.

It forced us to form a semicircle around him like children listening to a story, but none of us minded. Far from making himself the center of attention, he acted more like the sun, radiating friendship out in all directions equally.

As leader, it fell to me to cut the party short and bring up the reason we had come. To their credit, the brother and sister dropped everything they were doing to listen as soon as the tone turned serious.

Gracie pulled up a chair and looked at me with an intensity that put me a little off balance. She was a truly beautiful woman, it was true. But I had seen ravishing beauties through the ages. It was her focus and intelligence that made me feel a connection to her as we got down to business.

Matt even sat up and leaned forward. That was the first time that I suspected that his laid back, lazy persona was a show. The eyes that studied me were somber and intelligent. He took the lead in the discussion, answering my questions.

"Do the two of you remember Humeer?"

"Yup, he showed up shawtly after we did. He brung a lot t' the school, but we never really got friendly," Matt admitted. "He's in some sort a trouble, right?"

"Have you heard something?"

"Wahl, Tory, Ah don't need to bend mah ear t' gossip t' know mah cow's eatin' grass, do Ah? Just its nature, is all. Humeer's t' sort t' seek trouble an he's quick enough t' find it."

"You're certainly right about that, Matt. And the kind of trouble he's in is the kind that spreads."

"Figgered so." Matt nodded along.

"We need to stop him, and we need your help."

"Ah follow ya, friend of Aegon; but what yer not tellin' me is why t' rest of yer friends are lookin' so sad 'bout it. Ah'd surely like to hear that part first, iffn' ya don't mind."

"Humeer has been killing people to strengthen his magic. He has already grown very powerful and has already massacred the rest of the school." I knew enough about people to know that these two could handle the truth, without dilution. Still, a horrified gasp escaped Gracie.

"Dat right?" Matt looked to Aegon, who nodded. "That surprises me a little, but not lots, always a kinda darkness in t' boy. Ah take it he's not done, ya?"

"Hardly, and that is why we've come to you. He has thirteen others with him. They have already been slaughtering people like cattle on the other side of the mountain, and we figure it won't be long before they show up here."

"Suh, Aegon musta told ya we didn't want no part of his magic, though we're grateful for t' help he gave us..."

"Of course we'll help," his sister interrupted, shooting a scathing look at her brother. "We're not about to stand by while innocents are murdered, not while there's something we could do."

"A' course, a' course!" Matt hurried to jump in, withering under the accusing look of his sister. "All Ah meant to say was we might not be as strong as them, but we'll do all we can, how 'bout?"

"That's all I can ask."

"See now, that leads me right t' my next question. Why you askin'? Now don't look at me all cross-eyed, sis, Ah didn't mean it like that. Ah mean, Aegon's sittin' right there where Ah could reach out an' slap 'im iffn Ah had a mind to; why you askin' an' not him?"

"Oh he's the leader of all of this." Aegon jumped in gleefully to supply the information, a devilish grin on his face. "He's going to be making the plans and giving the orders."

"An' you trust 'im? You?" Matt was incredulous.

"Trust or not, he's the very best chance we got of any of us coming out of this alive." The sorcerer's grin was gone and he was deadly serious. It was good enough for Matt and Gracie.

"Never thought Ah would see a day when you handed reins t' somebody else, Aegon. This must be some kinda man. Though Ah would love t' know why he makes my skin crawl."

"Matt!" Gracie scolded, shocked at her brother's bad manners. "These are guests in our home, show some respect!"

"Ah have all kinds and flavors of respect for t' man, Gracie. Anybody who can win a 'yessir' from Aegon deserves all t' respect Ah can dig up, but ya can't tell me you don't feel it too. Sometin's not right about this boy."

Gracie met my eyes for just a moment, blushed, and turned away. She had a very pretty blush.

"All the same, Matt, it's not the kind of thing you bring up."

"Ah don't see why not, we're signin' up t' go die with 'im, seems like Ah got all t' reason in t' world for askin'."

"Your brother's right, Gracie," I interceded as she was about to scold him again. "I am asking you to put your lives in danger. You can ask all the questions you want, for now, anyway. There may come a time when I need you to obey without question. So now is certainly the time.

"He's doubly right in that there is something different about me. If I didn't tell you myself, Aegon would. I'm surprised he hasn't already made some kind of insult about it already. I am a Historian. The reason it feels unnatural when you look at me is because your magic allows you to sense that I am not entirely mortal."

Chapter 11

It is impossible to know the whole depth of someone's character from a single moment, but seeing how they respond to the unexpected is a great start.

–Musings of the Historian

"Not entirely mortal," Matt repeated. "Ah never knew such things came in shades. Perhaps you would like t' explain that a little more, how 'bout?"

"I can't die, at least as far as I know. I walk over thousands of worlds as a witness to great stories. I don't know how it works or what I was before, or if there even was a before. I'm here now to witness this story."

"Leadin' ain't witnessin'" Matt observed drily.

"You are absolutely right about that. This story is different, and I've had to involve myself."

"My, but we are special." Matt smiled. "Now Aegon, this ain't t' first time Ah've felt this. Right when you first pulled us in, you were saying goodbye to somebody. He felt wrong too, though he wasn't around long. What did we call him? Riggan? Reelan? Somethin' like that."

"We called him Rayan, though that wasn't his name," Aegon said glumly, knowing that some of his precious information had slipped. I didn't let it slide by.

"Your story was witnessed by a Historian. He was there when you figured out how to use the magic." It wasn't a question. "That's how you know about me."

"Yes," he admitted, but offered no further explanation.

"What do we need to do?" Gracie moved the conversation forward.

"I have some ideas of how we might beat them, but our odds aren't very good in any of them," I confessed. "We need to come up with our own advantage."

"Well why didn't I think of that, Master?" Aegon snapped. "What makes you think there's anything else? Unless you mean for us to start twisting our souls like they do, you heartless dung."

"Far from it, my smoky friend. Even if everyone was willing, they have numbers and a head start. We'd never match them with their own methods. We need something of our own."

"What do you suggest?" Gracie asked in earnest. "I know that people in the school have tried for years to understand it better, only Humeer did it. Does your immortality give you knowledge about our magic that could help us?"

She impulsively put her hand on my knee and I found myself wondering if it were possible for a Historian to blush.

"No, I have never encountered your magic before, though I have seen a great many kinds of magic. Most of all, I've learned to keep my eyes open. I've already seen some things that could use a closer look."

"Such as?" Aegon snapped again, impatient.

"Why don't you burn?" I asked him. He proffered his scarred

arms like an exhibit.

"Of course I burn, you numbskull! These aren't freckles, you know. I might have expected something that insanely stupid from the farmer, but not you."

"Shut up, Aegon, and listen. You've got burns, yes, but I've seen you in flames that would have scorched your whole body black. Just the flames that came off of Edana when you were unlocking her magic would have burned the arms off of you. Magic and science are never that far apart, where does all the extra energy go?"

"You..." He had already revved up with a new string of insults, it was instinctual for him. But as the sense of what I said sunk in, he trailed off and pondered the question. After a couple seconds, he shrugged.

"I guess I don't know. I never thought about it like that. I figured my own magic protected me, but I've even been protected when my fire was completely gone out of me. If anything, the protection was the strongest then. Though it's not like armor or anything, I still burn."

"When you were doing battle with your student out in the wilderness, when I first saw you, how much fire were you able to produce? More than usual?"

"I was fighting for my life, you goat kissing manure shovel, I didn't really notice!"

"I say it was more than usual," I stated. The battle had raged all the whole time I had been walking up to him, with intense flame being thrown back and forth. I had a fair idea of how much magic could be stored in a person from the display of all of Edana's magic being drained from her at one time.

"Ok, so it was more than usual, as long as you say so, Master. What's your point?"

"Could someone else recharge your magic with their own?"

"I suppose it's possible," he mused. "Though I can't see what use that would be. The effects would be temporary, they'd still burn, and we still wouldn't have any more power as a group."

"Let me worry about that," I assured him. "The first thing we need to do is to find out if I'm right."

"Ya need me t' burn 'im?" Matt offered eagerly, a smile on his face. Aegon glared at him.

"Probably, but we need to figure out how much he can take. If he can absorb a trickle without being burned at all, that would be best. Also, we would want to know if he can absorb from multiple people, or if it would just add up and fry him. It's time to apply science to this magic."

"Why is everybody assuming that it has to be me?" Aegon whined. "Seems like any of us could absorb magic. Why don't we start with Edana? She's just been drained, seems like she'd be a prime candidate."

"No," I insisted. "It has to be you. You have the most control over the magic of anyone here. You are also the ultimate target for Humeer and his group. I'm sure any one of them would love to have a shot at killing their teacher. Imagine what that would do for them. I suspect they also see you as their last remaining threat. With you out of the way, they can rule as gods in this world."

"So I'm to be the bait?"

"Just about."

"Great."

The testing started immediately. Aegon grumbled and whined about being tortured for people he'd just as soon kill himself, but he didn't hesitate to set up the experiment, baring his back to the group and leaning over a fence. He looked like a criminal, subjecting himself to a whipping. I guess the analogy wasn't far off of the truth.

"We need to establish a baseline first, Aegon. I need you to use up all the magic within you, so we can see if you gain any from the others."

"You know that will leave me defenseless, right? Or is that part of your brilliant plan to cripple your best shot at winning this?"

"Oh stop whining, you big baby. We are far from the mountains, there's no reason to believe that they have made their move yet, and we have others here to help. On top of all of that, I don't actually care whether you like it or not, you promised to follow along."

"Yes, Master," he grumbled sarcastically. His expression shifted and a disturbing smile twisted his face and he unleashed a burning bolt of flame right at my chest. The others in our group jumped back, gasping. Gracie screamed.

Her horror turned quickly to bewilderment when she realized that I wasn't burning. Only Altur, who had seen me stabbed with a red hot blade, looked unimpressed. The flames hammered at me as Aegon poured all of his raw emotion into it. Screwing his face into a pinched look of concentration, he focused the gout of flame into a thin thread which burned white with heat.

I could feel the heat of it, I could even feel the burn of it. In truth, I could feel everything that was done to me, I had even felt the knife plunge into my chest during Aegon's first demonstration. The difference was that the pain felt like it was happening to someone else.

The white ribbon of flame finally dimmed to the normal yellows and reds as Aegon's concentration faltered with his failing magic. I stood in the inferno for a minute longer as he worked to completely channel any magic he had left in his mind.

With a final flick of his wrist, he sent one last puff of flame, right into my face. I blinked and coughed, the biggest reaction he had got from me. He nodded, all smiles.

"There you go, Master, that's all of it."

"Great, now you can lean over the fence, good boy," I shot back. He responded with an insulting gesture, but he turned and once again draped himself over the rail.

"Matt, would you...?" My question died on my lips as I turned to address the rest of them. Their faces were a mixture of awe, confusion, and fear. For some reason, it made me feel particularly bad to see Gracie look at me with fear in her eyes. She looked like she was ready to run away or attack if I made any sudden moves.

"It's all right," I said in soothing tones. "We already discussed this. I can't die, I don't know why. Aegon just likes to throw it in my face that he knows about me and there's nothing I can do to stop him from telling people."

"Ah get why he's that way, suh. Ah have known Aegon long enough t'know he likes to get under the skin of people. What's got me head scratchin' is how you came t'be this way. Makes a man skittish hearing that Humeer and his troop are getting stronger through killin', then seein' something like that. What sort of things must you have done?"

"Hey now, I haven't hurt anybody," I promised. Aegon

snorted derisively behind me, still draped over the fence. They looked to him for a moment, but he offered no explanation.

"I am here to help." I tried a different tactic. "I know how strange it must be to see something like you just did. I wish I could give you an explanation, but I can't. If I did this to myself, I don't remember it. If it was done to me, I don't remember that either.

"I don't have magic, I can't throw fire. If what Aegon says is true, I can't even really hurt anybody. I know it's strange, but we need to move past it if we're going to deal with the problem we have right in front of us. Can you do that?"

Altur stepped forward. He trusted me the most and had already had time to process my mysterious nature.

"I'm with you, Tory. I don't know what you might have been or all that you are, but I feel that you are a good man. I know my opinion doesn't count for much..."

"That's right!" Aegon threw back from the fence.

"...seeing as I can't use magic like everyone else, but I agree with Aegon that you are our best shot of seeing another summer."

Finishing his speech, he was suddenly aware of standing all by himself and started fidgeting. Edana stepped forward to stand by him.

"I'll be honest," she began. "I don't really trust you. It's not personal, but everything is too bizarre for me to process right now. Unfortunately, it looks like I don't have the time. If we're really going to be overrun by evil magicians burning people with fire, then I don't mind saying I'd like to be standing by someone who can't be burned, trust or not."

I nodded, accepting her reservations along with her

commitment. Gracie shocked me by walking straight up to me, staring up at my face for a moment, then throwing her arms around me in a hug. I was so stunned I didn't even put my arms around her in return, not even so much as a back pat. I just stood there like an idiot. I heard Aegon chuckle at my obvious discomfort. She backed off, leaving her hands on my shoulders, her eyes on mine.

"I am so sorry for what has been done to you. I can't imagine what it must be like to live forever without a family. As long as you're here with us, we'll be your family, Tory."

She stepped back to stand with Altur and Edana. I was too overwhelmed to speak. I opened my mouth a time or two, to try and say thank you or at least tell her how much it meant to me, but nothing came out. Matt saved me with his characteristic practicality.

"Whatcha need done?"

Chapter 12

*Discovery has always been an act of imagination and will.
This holds true in all fields, be it magic, technology, or even
matters of the heart.*

–Musings of the Historian

"Go over to Aegon," I commanded, though my voice broke
ever so slightly as I did so. Luckily, the task at hand was delicate
enough that it soon demanded my attention entirely.

"I need the smallest amount of flame you can produce, throw
it at his back."

Obedient, Matt took a moment to focus. His magic wasn't
nearly as advanced as Aegon's, so the idea of creating a small puff of
flame and then stopping the flow was a monumental task of focus
and self-control. He even stood differently.

Every time I had seen Matt, he had been relaxed. Whether
walking, sitting, or standing, he always looked on the verge of
toppling right over as he expended the minimum amount of effort
possible to keep himself upright.

Now he stood with his feet just past shoulder width apart,
leaning forward in a stance of intense focus. The way he was staring
at Aegon's back, I half expected the fire to shoot from his eyes. The
rest of us stood in absolute silence as he took several long minutes to
prepare his mind. When he was finally ready, he lifted his hand and
a rather large ball of flame jumped out of his hand and slammed

into Aegon, who immediately burst into a pain-fueled tirade.

"Why in the blazes did you pick Matt?" he yelled at me. His back looked like it was sun burned from the overly large ball of flame that had washed over him. "If Edana weren't here, I'd have called him the worst sorcerer in the group! I swear you do this on purpose, Historian. It's just a reflection of your dark, twisted little soul is what it is."

"For mercy's sake, Aegon, try your magic, would you?"

"Gladly!" His hand raised and a small, pitiful fireball rolled from his fingertips and washed gently over my face. I didn't even give him the satisfaction of a blink.

"So it worked," I stated. He nodded grudgingly.

"So what? We can turn a big fireball into a smaller fireball. I suspect with a bit of work, we could make a hatchet out of an axe too."

"We need to keep experimenting," I insisted. "Matt, do you think you could do a smaller one?"

"Umm... might be, might be. But Ah'm already a little taxed. Shutting it off is t' hard part, ya see. Takes a lot out of ya. Maybe Gracie could give a go, how 'bout?"

"Not yet. I understand that Gracie has more control, but that's exactly why I need her towards the end of these little experiments. To fine tune a process, you need fine tools."

"D'ya hear that, Gracie? The old man says you're a fine tool, Ah imagine he meant it as a compliment of sorts." Matt smiled back at her. A warm blush rose around her collar and she averted her eyes. I turned back to the task at hand, anxious to focus on something besides Gracie's blush.

"Try putting your hand on his back." The suggestion came from Altur, of all people. "You get the most heat right up against the stove, it stands to reason you might transfer more if so much wasn't warming the air."

"Lovely! Now the village idiot chimes in!" Aegon's eyes shot daggers at the farmer over his shoulder. "He even had a nice folksy analogy to go with it. I am so bloody thrilled that my back gets to be the burned hand in that little story, as I've no doubt that the farmer chanced upon this priceless wisdom after touching his stove for the tenth time to see if it was hot!"

"Do it." I smiled at Matt. The idea actually made a lot of sense, for all of Aegon's negative ranting about it. What we were trying to achieve was an energy transfer, and it was clear that our transfer method had a lot of flaws. On top of that, there was even precedent, Aegon had made direct contact with Edana to activate her magic. Perhaps he had been pumping magic into her inadvertently, adding floods to a reservoir that was already overflowing.

Matt stepped forward and placed his hand on Aegon's bare back. Aegon continued to grumble about farmers, idiots, and cold fingers as Matt once again summoned up his mental powers to try and control the magic so he didn't burn a hole clear through the other man's ribs.

"All right," Matt whispered. I was the only one close enough to hear and I noticed that in his focused state, he didn't have his usual accent. The tiniest flickers of flame danced around the edges of his fingers as he channeled fire directly onto Aegon's back. I hoped that a good transfer of magic was happening at the same time.

"Enough!" Aegon roared, shaking the other man away. "You clumsy sheep-sniffing hick! The next one's coming at your head!"

He staggered around for a moment, bending his torso this way and that, trying futilely to adjust his back so the bright red hand print on it didn't sting so much. It was a decent burn, and it looked like tiny blisters were already starting to form around the edges.

"You just about done?" I asked, purposefully drawing his anger back towards me and away from Matt. I was fairly sure that he hadn't been serious about throwing a fireball at Matt, but you could never be sure with Aegon, and it paid to be careful. The tactic seemed to work and he spat at me, refusing to speak until he was done.

"That was easier," Matt commented.

"How do you mean?"

"T'wasn't as hard t' stop." Now that the moment was over, his usual drawl had returned.

"I can't feel what you're feeling, Matt, you'll need to give me a better idea of what's going on."

"Ah'm not too good at bendin' words to where Ah need 'em, but Ah'll give a go. Maybe think about pushin' a cart. If'n it's runnin' downhill, it's gonna take a lot of effort to stop it once it gets started. But if'n it's goin' uphill, all you need t' do is stop pushin'. That clear?"

"You're saying that you could feel an opposing pressure to your magic?"

"I s'pose."

"Fascinating, we may be on to something here. Next time, let's try..."

I jumped instinctively as a large fireball washed over me, the heat from it slamming into me like a fist. I looked through my upraised arms at Aegon, who was still throwing fire at me, a wicked grin on his face. He was able to keep it up a full ten seconds before the flames died away.

"Now that was impressive," I commented. Even Aegon looked pleased at our progress. Of course, pleased was a foreign and disturbing emotion when seen on the sorcerer's face. Still, the enthusiasm was hard to dim. Even those on the sidelines wore smiles and shifted anxiously as they watched and waited. They didn't know the significance yet, but there was joy in discovery and everyone was caught up in it.

"How could we not have noticed this earlier?" Gracie wondered. "We spent so much time at the school studying this magic, but we never figured this out. It seems so obvious now."

"Things always seem obvious once they're out in the open. It's to your credit that you didn't discover this earlier. If you had been the types to be experimenting with burning each other, you'd be a lot more like Humeer."

"Indeed, so glad we have you on hand to lend a psychopath's perspective," Aegon cut in, not one to miss a chance to insult me. He went back over to the fence and leaned on it, ready for the next test. For all his grumbling, he was excited too. That's when I saw it.

The hand print on his back was still red, but it had faded to a dull red, not the bright angry red of just a minute or two before. The blisters were also gone. Somehow his own use of the magic had pulled a lot of the heat from the burn, like a sponge sopping up residual magic. It went a ways to explain Aegon's good mood that the burn had healed so much.

"New idea," I announced. "Gracie, I need you for this one."

She stepped up obediently and Matt slipped back in line

gratefully. I understood all too well, Aegon was volatile in the best of situations. Standing around burning him was a risky business, especially now that we had proved that it helped recharge his magic when done in a controlled manner.

"Gracie, I need you to put your hand on his back, channel some magic into him, and stop."

"Lovely new idea, Historian, where do you get these genius insights?" I ignored Aegon's sarcasm and pressed on.

"Aegon, once you have a bit in you, I want you to start casting a small, controlled flame, right in front of you. Gracie, once he has started, put your hand on his back and start channeling magic into him again. Everyone understand?"

Gracie nodded, Aegon snorted, and we began. The first part went like the previous time. Gracie left a smaller, feminine hand print burn on Aegon's back and the old man once again stomped around for a moment, cursing at everyone as his gray singed hair completed the perfect image of a madman. When he was done cursing, he leaned back on the fence, bringing his hands together. He looked to Gracie and nodded, then crafted a small ball of flame in between his hands.

I began to understand how much control over the magic could mean. The tiny, stationary ball was entirely different from the gouts of flame and rolling fireballs I had seen from the magic so far. The tiny sphere showed how much it could be controlled, even outside the sorcerer.

It made me wonder about the nature of the fire. It was becoming clear that it was linked to the caster, some extension of themselves. I didn't have long to ponder, however. Once he had the flame stable, dancing and rolling between his palms, Gracie stepped up and placed her hand on Aegon's back. A soft glow of flame surrounded her hand.

The ball of flame between Aegon's hands grew brighter, almost white with heat, like the ribbon he had shot at me the first time to drain his magic. His eyes glowed as he stared at it. It flickered and its shape twisted and distorted.

"Back it off just a bit," he whispered to Gracie. She nodded, though he couldn't have seen her. The flame stabilized and once again formed a neat glowing ball. Smiles grew on every face as two minutes ticked by, the ball of flame undisturbed.

"That's enough," Aegon said, but it wasn't the irritated command he had thrown at Matt. The glow around Gracie's hand stopped immediately, a testament to her superior control. When she drew her hand away, she left another small hand print on Aegon's back. This time, it wasn't red or angry, just the lingering shadow that comes of pressure and warmth.

"It didn't burn me," Aegon stated what was already clear to most of us.

"So if your magic is already flowing, you can process another person's magic much easier, acting as a conduit for the energy, rather than trying to store it up. Now we're getting somewhere."

"Anything else you wanted to try?" Aegon's mood was much improved, having gone through an experiment that didn't involve another burn.

"That's enough for now. That gives me something I can use, but we'll need some time so everyone can recharge their magic. How long would it take for everyone to be back at near full capacity?"

"It's different for everybody. I'll be back to twitching within a couple days. Matt and Gracie here will likely take the better part of a week, if I remember right. Edana will be erratic as her mind and body try to adjust to what has happened to her. She could start overflowing in hours, or she could still be bone dry for weeks. She'll need the time before she could help with anything like that. Channeling a small flow like Gracie did isn't that hard, but it still takes tremendous focus."

"All right then. We can't take anything for granted. We'll settle in here until everyone's just below full strength. We'll need some time to travel and I don't want anyone starting to go crazy on me. In the meantime, we need to start a guard rotation. I can handle most of it, as I don't need to sleep, but I'll still need time in camp to get to know everybody."

"But of course, we wouldn't want to deny you your precious socializing."

"Shut up, Aegon. You know full well that we aren't going to win this like a regular war. You brought me on because I know human nature. That's not going to do us much good if I don't know my own team. I need to be able to predict what each person will do in any given situation. Considering that this is the first time I've ever done anything like this, I don't want to take any chances."

"This is the first time you've done this?" Gracie asked.

"This is the first time I've ever interfered in a story this much. The most I've done in the past is offer advice. Even that is seldom more than helping people commit to what they already wanted to do."

"Are you sure you can do it?" Her question was not a challenge. Her tone was concerned, worried about me.

"I honestly don't know. There is a fundamental part of myself that rebels against it, even now. Any action takes a lot of work because I'm fighting against my own nature."

"Why would you do that for us? Surely other people in your stories were just as deserving."

"I hate to admit it, but my interest here is a selfish one." I truly felt ashamed, especially telling it to her, but I couldn't bring myself to lie to her. "Aegon knows something about me, possibly where I came from. I have made a deal with him to help in exchange for the knowledge he has. Putting me in charge is his sick idea of a joke."

"Sounds about right," she replied, noticing Aegon grinning off to my left. "Well I hope you get what you're searching for. I'm glad you're helping us, Tory."

Her sincerity was disarming.

Chapter 13

There comes a time in every person's life when they ponder their own sanity. They poke and prod at the barrier that separates them from madness. This self-destructive tendency makes me wonder if there isn't some part of the thinking mind that would rather be insane.

–Musings of the Historian

I left the rest of them at the house to settle in and inventory our supplies and weapons, though it was obvious we didn't have nearly enough of either. I took the first watch and walked in ever-growing circles around the house, like a giant spiral on the ground. I noted hiding places, ambush spots, and the easiest paths to the house.

I wasn't expecting any attack. Humeer and his team didn't even know for sure that Aegon was still alive, and if they did, they would have no idea where he was; but the situation was bad enough without any surprises.

I had some ideas, and the situation wasn't nearly as dire as it seemed. It is easy to despair when faced by a superior power, but things are never simple. Great power creates instabilities, in nations and in men.

It is like a mighty fortress. It may seem indestructible by any army or bombardment, but all it takes is the timely application of water, acid, pressure, or excavation, at the right place, at the right time, and the whole thing will come crashing down under its own weight. Whether that fortress was a nation, a person's mind, or a literal fortress makes little difference, the principle is the same.

All that I needed to do was to find the right combination, the right pressure and the right time.

When I got back to camp, I selected Aegon for the next watch. He grumbled and swore at me, but he gathered his things, stuffing his pockets with dried meat to tide him over through the long night. I followed him out. He scowled at me.

"What do you want? I think I can figure out a lookout on an empty forest. I've spent my fair share of time in the woods."

"Yes, I get that feeling," I responded drily. "Today I advanced your understanding of your own magic, something you hadn't been able to do in years of study. I've done my part, I'm pushing this story forward. I think it's time you started to fulfill your part of the bargain."

"Oh you think that, do you?" he mocked, but he relented. "What do you want to know? I'm not going to give up everything, you understand. I've got to keep you on the leash somehow."

"I get that." He wasn't wrong. It was hard to interfere at this level. If he didn't have the information about my past hanging over my head, I didn't know that I would continue. "You were insane, weren't you? That's how you survived the madness, right?"

"What?" My line of questioning surprised him, as well as my insight into his own past. "You have been gagging yourself over what I know about you, Historian, and you would waste your first shot hearing my story? And what makes you think I was insane? For that matter, what makes you think I'm sane now?"

"I ask to hear your story first because right now it's the most relevant. I'm not interested in tidbits of what you know, I want the whole story, and the best chance I have of that is to know my team well enough to get us through all this alive.

"As for my suspicions on your sanity, there are a few clues, though I'm still waiting to have you confirm. First of all, there's your clothes. When I first saw your rough leathers, I thought that might just be the level of technology in this land, but meeting Altur set me straight quickly enough. These people have decent textiles, no reason to wrap yourself in animal skins.

"Besides, your student wore the same, the one you killed. I'm guessing they started copying you, their teacher. Am I right?"

"So far, what else you got?"

"Most of all, I have seen what this magic does to people's minds. I saw what it did to Edana. That level of mental anguish drives everyone it touches mad enough that they kill themselves. Altur hadn't heard of anyone surviving it, ever.

"So you were the first one ever, likely in hundreds of years, to master this thing. So you couldn't have been the same as everyone else. My guess is that you were completely insane, a savage in the hills, haunting caves. The madness didn't kill you because your brain was wired wrong, you couldn't even think straight enough to kill yourself. It burned inside you longer than it had in any other person until something broke and you unleashed the inferno. How am I doing?"

"Well you shouldn't wonder why nobody likes you, Historian, a know-it-all like you. I wonder why you even needed me here if you already knew the story. Yes, I wasn't living what you'd call a regular lifestyle when the madness hit."

"Tell me the story from the beginning," I prompted softly.

"Fine, but this is all you get for now. This makes us square for showing us the magic sharing, agreed?"

"Agreed."

"All right then. You need to understand that there are gaps in this story. I'm not holding out on you, I just don't remember them myself. The biggest gap is my life before the mountains. All I have are scenes and flashes.

"I remember fields and a farmhouse. I remember a woman and a boy child. I remember seeing them dead in the snow. I think they died in the cold, or maybe they were sick. I feel like it was my fault, like I was supposed to protect them. I know I should feel something about that, and I'm sure I did at the time, seeing what it led to. Now I can't remember enough of it to feel like it was real.

"It must have been all sorts of real at the time, though, because it broke my mind. I can only guess that I must have been fragile already, because people lose loved ones all the time, they don't go nuts. Doesn't matter much., T the point is, I did. I ran away from there until I couldn't run anymore, and that was the mountains. The solitude only added to the instability, though, and it wasn't long until I heard them."

"Heard who?" I nudged when his eyes grew distant and he seemed like he was about to stop talking.

"Voices, but more than voices, Historian. It was like they

were full people. I could only hear their voices, but it was like they were standing right behind me, like I could see them if I wanted to turn around."

"I've heard of mental disorders similar to that," I commented.

"Oh shut up. You haven't heard a story like mine, I promise. These voices kept me company through long nights and many seasons. After a while, they started to become part of me, or I became part of them, it's hard to be sure. All I knew was that it got hard to tell which voice was my own. It was like I had four or five people, all living inside one body. My reality was fluid. I was one person, then another. I was even a woman sometimes. It's easy to keep up those kinds of delusions when you've lived alone for years.

"All this time, I was living off the land, trapping varmints and rutting around for tubers like a swine. When I couldn't get something myself, I stole it from the settlements that were near the mountains. I think there was even one of them that thought I was a ghost or something like that.

"My mind was so far gone, I wasn't even surprised when one day there was a man sitting on a stump watching me. It was like he had always been there. I even wondered if maybe that's who I was, like looking at a reflection. For reasons I'll never understand, he stayed around, watching me. He later said he felt like there was going to be a story. It wasn't anything to him to wait around a year or two to see what might happen."

"I know the feeling," I interjected. "It's an instinct."

"Bah!" he scoffed. "It's a command, you're just too dumb to see it for what it is, but you haven't paid for that knowledge yet. Still, you're right, this new addition to my family of one was a Historian. Sure enough, there was a story brewing in me.

"It was only a few months later that there was a new feeling in my head, a pressure I couldn't push against. It just kept growing and growing. The voices in my head, the other people, the other versions of myself, screamed and writhed underneath it. I cycled between voices and personalities like spokes on a spinning wheel. Each one hated to be in the foreground, because it meant absolute anguish.

"Some tried to push back, to fight. Some tried to kill themselves, but things were so confused that my body was almost completely locked down as my mind burned and pulled itself apart. That was the beginning of it.

"I am not sure how long it went on. The turmoil became such that I was only slightly aware of my own existence. Though I have never drowned, I have heard that there comes a point when the world explodes in your mind and things like up and down become meaningless concepts. That is probably the best way I can describe it.

"While I heard later from the Historian that I was conscious through the whole ordeal, babbling, retching, and even chewing on things around the camp, I don't remember any of it past the confusion of clashing insanities.

"The last moment when I had any concept of what was around me, it was winter and my mind was melting as I screamed in the snow. The next thing I remember, I was sitting in flames as they scorched the walls of my cave, reflecting the heat back on me like a kiln.

"Breathing was hard as the smoke and heat choked me. I think if I'd been further into the cave, I would have died right then. Luckily, I was fairly close to the cave opening. I couldn't tell where the fire was coming from, but it was unbearable. I staggered out of the cave to get some air. It was summer.

"The last of the fire was still racing up and down my arms. I brushed at it, scared like an animal, but the flames wouldn't die and after a moment I realized that they weren't hurting me. The Historian followed me out of the cave, amazement on his face. He must have supplied at least a little food and water to keep me alive, though I had lost a lot of weight in the flash of lost time.

"My next shock came when I realized that I was alone. The Historian was there, just watching, but I was truly alone for the first time in years. My mind was quiet. The simplest thoughts skipped around in my empty skull like mice in an empty dining hall.

"In that moment, I was afraid. I certainly would never have chosen madness, coming from sanity; but when your reality is shaped by constant shifting inside your own mind, the sudden silence was almost too much to bear.

"I asked the Historian what had happened. He only blinked at me, amazed all over again. After a moment, he apologized and introduced himself as a lost traveler who had seen my camp and had wintered with me. It was a lousy lie, but I wasn't in any state of mind to be questioning someone else for their life choices. Looking back on it, he must have been pretty distracted himself.

"He explained that I hadn't said anything coherent for months. I had spoken incessantly, calling names, shouting nonsense, or just screaming into the air when I ran out of things to say. Apparently my lucid question had been as much of a shock to him as fire suddenly bursting from my every pore."

"I can imagine," I said. "Watching it happen to Edana was traumatic enough, I can't imagine what it must have been like to have it happen all of a sudden."

"Edana's release was nothing." His retort was condescending. "While I'm amazed that dumb farmer kept her alive that long, she was just barely at a point where her magic could be unlocked. Imagine her state if she had been kept alive for another four months."

I couldn't imagine. His psychosis must have been deep indeed. The madness must have filled every part of him before it finally burst free on its own. He continued.

"I considered myself cured. It seemed at the time that one madness had canceled out another. I was grateful, but still didn't feel ready to go back to regular society. The Historian tagged along after me as I started to take care of myself again. My body was gaunt, every rib showing as I had spent the winter surviving on little more than water and anything I managed to chew on or shove in my mouth, I think I ate a lot of tree bark.

"So I started trapping again. I used the skins to make myself some clothes, as I was scarcely better than naked in my old rags. I didn't have the tools for it, nor the experience to make anything decent, even if I had had the tools. The result is what you see before you, done with a needle made out of a sharpened rib from a rabbit.

"I even cut back my beard, which had grown almost to my belly button during my years living like a hermit. I couldn't shave, the knife I had stolen wasn't sharp enough for that, but at least I was able to make it look like it had been done on purpose.

"After some time had passed, the madness started to come back. This time there was only me, so I felt the pressure of it. The injustice of it was just too much, to recover from both sicknesses of the mind, just to relapse. I recoiled and lashed out at the world in my rage. To my immense surprise, I set myself on fire again.

"When the inferno had passed, the pressure was gone and I was myself again. That's when I began to understand the nature of the thing, that the fire was linked to the madness. It wasn't that hard of a thing to believe for someone like me, someone who had already had reality bend and shift like a leaf tossed about in the current of a river.

"After several talks with the Historian, who by then I considered my friend, my only friend, I decided that I could help people get over their own madness. It had been a problem with the people of this land for a long time, as long as anyone could remember. What better way to re-enter society than as a savior?

"I wandered from village to village. It didn't take long to find someone desperate enough to let me try. Their son was sick with the madness and had already tried to take his life once. They let me take him. I took him back to my cave and kept watch. The Historian helped, just as you were helping Altur. We fed him and kept him from killing himself. I even fed him some bark, just in case it was somehow tied to the release of magic.

"He made it another month before he bashed his head against a rock, ending his life. I still wouldn't be stopped. I cursed myself for carelessness, even blamed my wanderer friend at times, though he hadn't been on watch. I never doubted that others could do what I had done."

Aegon stopped and looked into my eyes. He took a deep breath before continuing.

"I want you to appreciate what I'm doing for you, Historian. I am telling you this story with only the facts, but I don't enjoy it. It sickens me to share my secrets with the likes of you. You'll smile and nod, you may even believe that you care, but you don't. I'm going to keep my end of the bargain, do what I said I'd do, but you should understand that I spit on your judging eyes and your immortal pity."

"Umm, ok, fair enough," I stammered, a little taken aback by the sudden hatred in his voice. My answer satisfied him though, he had said his piece and he trudged on through his story.

Chapter 14

Love truly makes the world turn, as it has been said. What people forget is that the turning of the world brings darkness as well as the light.

–Musings of the Historian

"I never told the boy's family. I was ashamed. I buried his body on the mountain without so much as a rock to mark the spot. For reasons I can't explain, the look of hope on their faces when I walked away with their son haunts me more than anything. Even watching him kill himself held little horror for me, only disappointment.

"Even after all this time, I can't think about their faces without getting a sick feeling in my stomach. It's the only thing that still can make me feel that way, and I've done some horrible things. I decided that I couldn't have any more such faces burning at my mind.

"After that, I just stole them. I would hear rumors of people going mad in other villages. The Historian and I would stake out the places, watching and learning. When the time was right, I would dart in, throw a bag over their head, and carry them off into the woods and back to the cave.

"I went through five more attempts that way. Five more

bodies stashed away on that mountain, but I never lost hope. That is the ultimate sickness, Historian, hope. Madness might make you do some crazy things, but hope will drive you to them, make you dedicate your life to things and blind you to the cost. Even after five more tries and six dead bodies, I was still convinced that I just wasn't waiting long enough. The problem was that I wasn't even getting close.

"Thanks to the Historian, I knew roughly how long it took for the madness to finally burst free of a person on its own. By my best estimate, the closest we ever got still had two months to go. We had even tied her down, even strapped her head to a board to keep her from smashing it against things. In the end, she figured out how to inhale at just the right moment to choke herself to death when we came to feed her. There is a kind of genius in madness, it seems."

"I have always said so," I added. He plowed on, ignoring me.

"It was on the next one that we had a breakthrough. The timing was just perfect. He had progressed almost to where the last one had died. We had him strapped to a board and only fed him soft mash. Still he managed to save enough in his cheeks, storing and packing the grains until he had a ball solid enough to block his throat, then he inhaled it.

"I knew as soon as I saw his lips turning blue that we had lost again. It happened during one of the times when the madness had started to creep back up on me. I'd like to blame it on that alone, but I can't. I was angry, I was frustrated, and he was dead anyway, at least in my mind.

"I grabbed him by the throat and shook him, screaming my rage at my impotence and his lunacy. The magic unleashed within me and I burned him, the magic coursing through my hands and into him. The shock of it actually managed to dislodge the ball in his throat and he breathed long enough to scream. Before I knew it, there was fire flowing back at me, another inferno like the one I had let loose on my first time.

"It was our first success, at least of a sort. He still died from what I had done to him. He died a sane man, horror in his eyes as he spent his last moments trying to make sense of where he was and what had happened to him. Luckily, it didn't last long, the wounds I had given him before his magic released were far too severe.

"It gave me the window of hope that I needed to keep going, twisted as it was. I hardened my heart to the horrors I had seen, to the pain I had caused. I buried another body and went looking for the next one.

"The body count rose as I buried another four bodies, pumping fire into them to unlock their magic. It took until the fifth attempt before I could pull my own magic back enough so as not to burn them to death in the process. That was my first student, a woman named Patty. Her burns were severe, and she bore the scars to her dying day, but she lived.

"After that, it was a matter of fine tuning the process. We collected more people who were suffering from the madness. We never had another fatality, though the first members were all horribly burned in the process.

"Being able to talk with people about it made a huge difference. We were able to compare what we felt when the madness came upon us, what we went through when it released. It didn't take long to figure out that pain was part of the unlocking and it didn't have to be magic.

"It was a bizarre moment, sitting and discussing how best to use torture to rapidly bring people to the breaking point where just a little push with the magic would break it free. We all felt that the ends justified the means, however, and we pressed on.

"For all their approval, no one else ever participated in the final process. The torture and burning was left entirely to me. Matt would sometimes help get them secured and get all of the implements ready, but he could never stand to stick around when the time came."

"Matt was there at the beginning?" I interrupted.

"Oh yes," he confirmed. "Matt was the fourth survivor. If you were to ever see him without his shirt, you would see angry burn scars all over his chest and stomach. I was still experimenting at that time with using my magic on different places on the body, trying to make the transition easier."

"And Gracie?"

"Gracie came later. We didn't actually expect the madness to fall on her, Gracie and Matt are the only case I have ever heard of where two from the same family were stricken with the madness.

"For reasons I'll never fully understand, the survivors stayed around after they had been 'cured.' I hadn't planned on starting a school, but that's how it happened. We would find someone with the madness, free the magic within them, and spend months out in the wilderness, just talking about the magic, experimenting with it, trying to make it stronger, trying to get more control.

"Most confusing was when they started dressing like me. I had made the animal skin clothing out of necessity; had I known how to make real clothes, or thought to steal some, I would have, it just wasn't important enough to me. They took to it like some kind of uniform. I guess it helps people to feel like part of a group to dress the same."

"Oh yes," I confirmed.

"Humeer came in at about number twenty. Shortly after that, a few of the older students decided to return to their normal lives, Matt and Gracie among them. What happened next, you've already heard. Humeer was the beginning of the end. His genius transformed the magic, made it better for all of us, but his ambition twisted it into something monstrous.

"Now I get to watch as the fruits of my hope tear this people down to be butchered and enslaved. That is hope for you, Historian, that is how one freak mistake, one lunatic in a cave can set in motion endless suffering because he doesn't know how to leave well enough alone."

"We might win," I offered. "You can't claim to have lost the war when you've only lost one battle."

"Don't you see?" he pressed, his eyes suddenly wild. In that moment, I could see him as the demented lunatic, living in a cave and gnawing on trees. "My true insanity lives on. The voices and the magic weren't what made me dangerous. This is what makes me capable of such atrocities: hope.

"I am a fool to keep on hoping, it has only led to greater and greater horrors. I asked for your help, but you are a burning poker in my eyes every time I see you. With you here, I still hope, clinging to some wispy possibility that I might turn this all around. You keep my head in this filth as sure as if you were holding my head under water."

He scowled his hatred at me and I knew that the story was at an end. Pressing my luck, I asked one more question.

"What happened to the Historian?"

"Wouldn't you just love to know? Forget it. I'll tell you that when we've got a plan that has a chance of working. In order to keep you on the line, though, I will tell you that he wasn't a Historian after that."

"What? Tell me what you mean by that. Tell me!"

I packed all the authority and power I had learned from kings, emperors and prophets into the command, but he just smiled gleefully. He had me and he knew it.

"You've had your story for the night. I'm going to bed, but I'll let you finish out my watch for me. Good night."

He walked back to the house and I was left alone in the darkness once more. What could he have meant? For a moment, I toyed with the idea that he might have been lying, messing with my mind to keep me committed to his little war. I had to dismiss it, though. A Historian knew a lie when he heard it. Even if there weren't centuries of experience at my command, I had always had an instinct for when people were lying to me.

So I was left with a thousand questions and no answers. Had the Historian in his story died? Was there something on this world that could kill me? Would I even avoid it if it came for me?

These questions and more plagued me through the night so I didn't even notice the passage of time. I was so disturbed that an entire army with torches probably could have walked into the house without me noticing. I was grateful when Matt found me and relieved me of the watch.

I knew I would get nothing more out of Aegon, but I couldn't stop turning things over in my mind. I needed a distraction. I knew just how to get it, too. Nothing distracts a Historian like a story. I sought out Edana, pulling her away from the group and sitting her down on a log. I sat on a nearby stump, an attentive listener.

"I'd like to know the last thing you remember before you awoke in Aegon's shack," I started. She swallowed nervously, still not comfortable around me. She was resolved, however, and dug deep to fulfill my wishes.

"It was just any other day. I had been feeling poorly for a long time. I was irritated at something. No, I guess that's not right, I was irritated at everything. I was bothered if the wind blew and it bothered me when it stopped. It built up until everything around me angered me. Every color hurt my eyes, but the darkness held demons for my imagination.

"I can't tell you a specific day, it just became too much. The last thing I remember was wanting to end it all, to stop feeling at any cost. The next thing I remember was waking up, chained to that wall. I was scared, of course, but it wasn't nearly as bad as what I was going through before."

"Thank you for telling me." I made sure that my stance, my voice, and every part of my body language communicated friendship. With the right nods and fidgets, at just the right times, a man can look entirely harmless, but without looking weak. "Have you been told what happened since then?"

"Not really, but I have heard plenty of stories about what happens to those with the madness. I would imagine I would have tried to kill myself if Aegon hadn't intervened."

"You did try," I told her. I wasn't all that surprised that she hadn't heard. Matt and Gracie didn't know, Aegon didn't care, and

Altur wouldn't tell a story like that, not to her. Surprise showed on her face.

"What did I do? Why am I not dead?"

"You tried to drown yourself in the river. Altur pulled you out, he kept guard over you day and night for a month. Aegon kidnapped you right from under his nose. The two of us chased him through the woods. Altur tackled him and convinced him to let us come along, once he knew that Aegon meant to help, that is."

She took a moment to digest this new information. Something didn't seem to add up for her., I had my suspicions about what was troubling her. Her next words confirmed them.

"Altur did all that?" Her words fairly oozed with disbelief.

"He is your husband." I said it as a statement, but meant it as a question. She dismissed it with a scoff.

"That's because of the laws in this land. It was my father's farm, you see. Altur has been a farm hand, working for my father, as long as I can remember. He's a good worker, don't get me wrong, but he was never more than that until my father died suddenly. His heart stopped, right there at the dinner table. He had seemed uncomfortable all day, but my father was never one to complain.

"He was barely cold in the ground before men from the village came out to ask me what I intended to do. I know you're not from this land, but here, single women can't own land, certainly not a farm. People here believe that a single woman with land to her name would become a target for those looking to take advantage of her situation. I've heard that there are men who can get quite inventive when it comes to persuading women to do what they want.

"I wasn't about to let my farm fall into a public trust. They would have taken care of me until I found a husband, it would be the least they could do in exchange for me losing my farm. Still, it was my family's farm, my home. So I called in Altur. The other two farm hands had left almost immediately after father had died, seeing that the farm was likely to fail. I instructed him to marry me so I could keep the farm, he obeyed. It was as simple as that.

"There was a little fuss from the villagers, those that smelled a trick, but legally there was nothing they could do. A newcomer argued that maybe Altur was already taking advantage and forcing me to marry him. The other villagers shut that down pretty quick, they all knew that Altur wasn't capable of something like that."

"So it was a marriage of convenience," I summed up for her. She shrugged and nodded. "Do you know why Altur stayed around while the other hands left? If he was such a good worker, he surely could have gotten a job somewhere else, maybe on a bigger farm."

"Good ol' Altur, that's what father always called him. He's loyal to a fault, and always looked up to father. Even when the work in the fields was done, he would still hang around the house, just in case father needed him for anything. I suppose father's death must have been really hard on him, too."

I had my own ideas about Altur's loyal attentiveness around the house. There couldn't be a more classic story than the hard working farm hand falling in love with the farmer's daughter. Only this time, it didn't end with happy smiles and scads of fat babies. She couldn't even see what was staring her right in the face, literally, at times.

I considered letting the matter go, it certainly would have been the easiest way to go; it was what I was accustomed to, observation. My conversation with Aegon still plagued me, though,

114

and the last thing I wanted was more time to myself. So I summoned up the will it took to actively interfere in a story and jumped in.

"Edana, have you wondered why he stuck around after the madness came upon you? Until Aegon came out of the woods, no one in your village had even heard of someone surviving it. Why do you think he stayed?"

"Oh he's just..." She trailed off, realizing that her simplistic answer didn't really fit the situation. "I guess he just didn't want to see me die, he's a good man, I'm sure he still feels some loyalty for my father, wouldn't want to have his daughter die."

"Your father is dead," I pressed, a little too harshly, perhaps, but my head was on fire from my interference in the story. "There was nothing he could have done to save you. No one would have blamed him if he had just walked away, or let you drown yourself. Many would have called it an act of mercy."

"I don't know!" she snapped back at me. It wasn't much of a retort, but she was upset with me for how roughly I had treated the subject of her dead father. "Maybe he's just dumb, like Aegon says!"

"Don't be a fool, Edana. I've spent a lot of time with Altur, and he is no fool. For all his insults, even Aegon has admitted some respect for him during honest moments. I doubt I even have to tell you this. I'm certain that you've had lots of opportunities to talk with Altur, after all, the two of you grew up together. Do you think he's stupid?"

"No, I know he's not," she admitted, though she still threw it back at me like an insult. "But I don't appreciate being called a fool, I don't care how old and wise you are! What are you trying to tell me? Why can't you just talk plainly?"

"Hazards of the job, I guess. I'm not going to tell you anything if you can't piece it together by now. I'll call you a fool if it suits me, Edana, I don't answer to anyone here, least of all you. Until you can tell me what I've been trying to tell you, the fool comment stands. Most women have an amazing instinct for these things, I'm not sure how you've managed to miss it all these years."

It was rude and abrupt, just as I had planned. It would create the dynamic I wanted. True to form, she stormed off without another word, fuming and furious. When the bright anger cooled into a nice grudge, she would put everything into figuring out the mystery I had put before her. She wouldn't want to, but she'd have no choice.

I had heard in her voice the devotion she felt for her father. She was the kind to idolize her father as a king, a convenient belief for girls who want to think themselves princesses. Her drive to please her father would translate into an urge to be her best for authority figures. My disapproval of her would burn like a father's scolding. Her very nature would force her to dwell on our conversation until she found out how to get back in my good graces.

Chapter 15

*Anyone can act strategically, it doesn't take much to make
a plan. The skill of a general is his or her ability to react
strategically when plans fail.*
       –Musings of the Historian

Edana passed Gracie coming the other way. Gracie said some
warm word of greeting I didn't quite catch, but Edana stormed right
on past. Gracie turned a puzzled look onto me and walked over to
satisfy her curiosity. She sat down on the log Edana had just vacated,
but sat much closer to the stump where I was sitting, so close she
could have reached out and touched my knee.

"What made her so angry?" she asked me, her clear blue eyes
searching my face.

"Indirectly, being raised as the only child of a doting father.
Directly, I called her a fool."

Gracie laughed, a light, tinkling sound that made me think
of wind chimes.

"I'm guessing you were talking about Altur?"

"You're very observant."

"Pshaw," she scoffed. "Anybody with eyes can see how he
follows her around like a moonstruck calf. Everyone except her, that
is. Are they really married?"

"Turns out they are, but it was just so she could keep her daddy's farm."

"Got it. Getting a feel for interference, are we?" she teased. "Does it make you uncomfortable to go from simple observer to master manipulator?"

Her words stung me a little, but I saw the truth in them. I had used my knowledge and experience to play Edana's mind like a harp, plucking strings where it suited me. I suddenly felt very guilty.

"Yes, more than you know," I admitted honestly. "It feels like I'm fighting something every time I put myself into the story line."

"Walk with me," she commanded and stood up. I hastened to my feet to walk with her.

"Where are we going?"

"There's a village just up the river. We weren't expecting visitors, so we don't have enough food to feed everybody. Also, if we're going to be traveling and fighting, we have the wrong kinds of food. So I'm going into town to pick up supplies and some food that can sit in a pack all day and still be edible at night.

"I was only going to talk to you for a second, but now I have more questions for you, so you can come along and help me carry everything back."

I smiled at her honesty. She was the first one to turn the tables on me, seeking information about me before I had the chance to quiz her about her own life with Matt.

"Ok then, ask away, but I have to tell you I don't know much about my own past."

"So you say," she started. "Haven't you ever interfered in other stories before? Surely there must have been some tempting moments. Surely there must have been times when you could have acted to save somebody, somebody you cared about?"

"I've never interfered on this level," I explained. "A story has its own structure, like a tree. Each decision by each person creates more decisions and the whole thing takes shape as all the decisions intertwine.

"The moments where I've interfered before have been miniscule things, a nudge at a twig. The big decisions that affected the shape of the story were always made by the true participants. Now I find myself right at the very trunk, the core of the story. I'm not witnessing this story, I'm making it."

"Is that such a bad thing? I understand that you aren't like the rest of us, but you still look and sound like a man. Men are supposed to feel the urge to shape their own story."

"It's not my story," I insisted. "That's the problem. This story doesn't belong to me. It isn't my battle, it isn't about my friends, and it isn't even my world. Everything I do here feels foreign, wrong in a way. Even if I want to make a change, there is something inside me that rebels at how unnatural it is. Now if I ever figure out what my own story is, I'd guess it would be another matter entirely."

"I suppose that makes sense in a way," she conceded. "I hope it doesn't cause you too much discomfort."

"It's manageable. Right now, not much has happened, so my interference has still been minimal."

"Well I appreciate it," she said, putting her hand on my shoulder for a moment. I was all too aware of the warmth of her small hand, a physical reflection of the warmth in her smile. I couldn't help but smile back.

"I hope I don't let you down," I said, realizing that I meant it. "You know this could still end very badly, we're outnumbered and outgunned."

"Of course, but we have to try. If we didn't, what sort of people would we be?"

The question hung in the air and we walked in silence. Her hand moved down off my shoulder and settled onto my forearm. It stayed there.

She had a swinging walk that covered ground quickly and I didn't have to think about slowing myself down to match her. It wasn't really until we arrived in the village that it hit me just how much I had been enjoying myself.

Gracie made her way to a building that could only have been a supply store. Sacks of grain lined one wall, a wooden floor and an overhang protecting them from the weather. Various farm tools were visible in the back.

As we walked in, Gracie made her way directly to the counter and started explaining her order to the man behind the counter. She was focused on her task and didn't seem to notice what was going on in the room behind her.

The room was filled with men, mostly farmers, by the look of them. They were arguing fiercely amongst themselves, pointing and glancing about as if they expected an attack. These were frightened men. These were the kind of men who spent their lives facing down storms, droughts, predators and disease almost every day.

The life of a farmer was spent under a constant threat of death. Whatever had frightened these men must have been something pretty severe. I made my way over to their group to listen

120

in on their fractured conversation, as each man talked over another.

"...can't just leave, I'd rather..."

"...fire from their hands, burning like..."

"...we leave now, maybe we..."

"...believe they're gods, that's what..."

"...less than a day, too close for..."

"ENOUGH!" I roared, cutting through the chatter of conversation. Out of the corner of my eye I saw Gracie spin around, snatching up a garden hoe in one hand, ready for an attack. The men stood and stared at me, shocked by the sudden interruption.

"I need you men to tell me, right now, what is going on."

They erupted into incoherent babbling as they all tried to answer at once.

"STOP! You, explain, quickly." I pointed to one of the farmers, a short man who was busy wringing his hat in his hands.

"You see, there's been an attack at the village north of us, near the mountains. A man was through here earlier today, said he escaped and was running south. Some of us think he might have been mad, but Ben here says that he's seen him before at socials and the like, said he was a dependable guy. But he's talking about fires and magic and gods."

"How many?" I demanded. The poor farmer stammered, confused at my question. I moved to clarify. "How many of these flame wielding gods attacked the village, and are they still there?"

"Umm, two, umm, sir?" It was a question more than a statement. He recognized my authority instinctively, as I was laying it on pretty thick, but he was still completely lost as to why or how he should respond. "The man said that there was two of them, and they were rounding people up. I suspect it's going on right now. We need to decide what we're going to do."

The farmer looked at me expectantly, but I had no time for him. I turned to Gracie.

"Get back as fast as you can, bring everyone here."

She wasted no time with questions, darting out the door and disappearing down the street. I turned back to the frightened farmers.

"There are powers at work here that are beyond you. I may need your help later, but right now, there's nothing you can do. Take your families, head south, away from the mountains. Warn the other people, tell them to gather whatever weapons they can get their hands on, but don't attack until you hear from me. Don't even try to defend your farms, just run."

An authoritative voice is a cool balm on frightened hearts. They scattered from the store, running in all directions to gather their friends and loved ones. I had no doubt that the village would be completely empty by nightfall.

If my plan worked, their evacuation would be entirely unnecessary, but I couldn't take that chance. Just two attacking meant twelve more out there somewhere. Other villages might be being attacked already and I would have no way to know.

Using regular farm folk as soldiers was a contingency plan I desperately wanted to avoid, but if it came to that, it would be better if the people were safe, gathered together, and used to taking orders from me.

I had hoped to have more time to prepare, but war had already come to the valley. That meant that the sorcerers thought that they were strong enough to pull it off and that didn't bode well for my small team. There would be no more time to gather other people or work more on developing the magic. I had to make do with what I had.

I turned to leave the store and almost tripped over the short farmer. He had initially started to scatter with the others, but had turned back. His hat still turned nervous cycles in his hands.

"Are they gods, sir?" His voice shook a little as he asked his innocent question. "We have stories, myths and stuff like that, but nobody has ever taken them seriously."

"No, they're not gods," I reassured him. "They have power and they are dangerous, and you should certainly steer clear of them, but they are human, just like you. I have it on good authority that one of them has already been killed."

"Oh." The hat stood still for a second as he looked up at me. "Are you?"

"What?"

"Are you a god, sir?"

I must have laid it on a little too thick.

Chapter 16

*Fear sticks like a barb in the mind. Someone cold enough
to take advantage of it can attach strings to those barbs and make
puppets of men and women.*

–Musings of the Historian

The others ran into town less than a half hour later. Gracie
must have run like a gazelle to have gotten to them so quickly. All of
them were puffing and heaving as they came into town, having run
almost the whole way at my command. Most of them were carrying
packs. Not knowing what the emergency was, it seems that they had
left under the assumption that they wouldn't be coming back. I
hoped it wasn't true, but it was far too early to say.

"What's going on?" Altur managed to gasp between heaving
breaths.

"There's been an attack on a village north of here." I briefed
them as they caught their breath. "I would have liked to have been
more prepared, but our time is up. We are going to war. As I
understand it, there are only two of them."

"Ah reckon... we could take two," Matt offered, still panting.

"I expect we could, but that wouldn't give us what we need."

"Now what do..."

"Shut up, Aegon. This is what you brought me in for and

there is no time to waste. I will explain when I have a chance, but for now, we need to move and move quickly.

"Does anyone know the layout of the village being attacked? Is it close to your farm, Altur?"

"No, Tory. Our village was on the other side of the river and further back into the woods. If they didn't know it was there, they probably missed it coming south."

"Then I need you to head north to that village. Don't let anyone see you, but I need you to find me a rough barn, right close to town, or a short wall. Once you've found a good spot and got the lay of the town, head south and meet us on the road. I'll need you to draw me a map. Go now, leave your pack, we'll bring it along. You need to move fast, as fast as you can. Understand?"

He nodded and dropped his pack. I knew the kind of endurance he was capable of. It was possible that one of the others would have been better, but the heat of battle was no time to take chances. He ran north out of town, his chest puffing like a bellows.

He was in this to save Edana, it was all he thought about. I knew he would run until his heart burst if it meant she would live. Gracie's words about manipulation struck at me again, but I had no time to consider the morality of my situation.

"Grab the rest of the packs, we'll need to move quickly too, but we can't be exhausted. All of you will need to use your magic in a controlled fashion. , I need you to be ready."

To their credit, they all nodded and shouldered their packs. I picked up the one Altur had dropped and slung it over my shoulder. We started off north at a quick march. I filled them in on the plan as best I could as we walked.

We stopped once we were out of sight of the village and were alone on the road.

"Edana is going to need a little magic for this," I explained. "Gracie, if you would, please."

The rest of us turned our backs so that Gracie could modestly unbutton a couple of the buttons on the back of Edana's farm dress and slip her hand inside, channeling a small amount of fire directly onto her back. Edana gasped at the first contact, then whimpered ever so slightly at the pain of it. Luckily, it didn't last long, Gracie knew that she would need plenty of her own magic to deal with what was ahead.

This was the other reason I had sent Altur on ahead, I know he wouldn't have liked that we had to put his wife into battle so quickly, especially as we had to burn her a little to get her enough magic to work with. Luckily, Matt and Aegon had been speaking with her about the mental techniques necessary to unleash her magic again.

Our preparations and instructions done, we continued on our way. Altur met us when we were still several miles outside of the town. His face was flushed and his shirt was fairly drenched with sweat from his forced run to the village. Out of breath, he explained as best he could while he drew an outline of the village in the dust that covered the road.

It was a decent setup, I decided. It could have been a little better, but it could have been lots worse. The buildings lined both sides of the road, mostly small business or large homes of the prominent citizens. Many of those were already in flames, Altur explained.

He confirmed that there were just two of them, dressed like

Aegon. They had herded the people together like cattle near the center of town. They would occasionally make another display of their magic, setting a house on fire or burning one of the citizens. Then they would allow one of them to leave, sending them in different directions.

It was an obvious tactic. They had no real interest in taking over this particular village, it was just convenient, likely the first one they had chanced upon. Their real aim was domination over all the people living in the valley, tens of thousands of people spread over hundreds of little villages and hamlets.

Psychological warfare was the aim of their first strike, a big display of force, letting plenty of people go to spread the word of their magic. If the village we had passed were any indication, they would soon have the whole valley quivering in fear, willing to submit to slavery rather than face a certain fiery death.

Luckily for us, they were taking their time with it, using their magic in tiny doses to great effect, spreading it out over a full day to give the impression that their powers were limitless. If they had coasted through the village just burning everything, they would have been long gone and we'd be chasing them.

"Edana, I need you there." I indicated a woodshed on the north end of town, an outbuilding next to a corral. Altur said they hadn't burned it yet or even gone close, likely not an impressive enough target. "Altur, you can go with her, but don't go inside the shed. Wait outside, then help her get away, back behind the buildings, here. You should be out of sight on the way back to me, I'll be here."

"What are you going to be doing?" Altur asked.

"Nothing at all, it's not my time yet."

"Sure, makes sense." Aegon couldn't let the opportunity for sarcasm pass. "The one person who can't die had better hide."

"My time will come," I assured them all. "But this all needs to happen in a certain order. We can't win this in one battle, or any number of battles, for that matter. My plan needs to build, step by step.

"Aegon, when the time comes, put yourself here, leaning up against this stone wall at the south. Everybody know what you're doing?"

They all nodded. Altur hadn't been with us on the road to hear the whole plan, but he didn't care past his role of guardian for Edana. Even those who knew the plan didn't understand the why of it, but the time for those kinds of questions had passed.

We snuck into the south end of town and everyone got into position. Edana and Altur worked their way around the outside of the buildings to the north end of town and the woodshed. Most of the buildings in town were now burning, which turned out to be a good thing. The massive fires had created a very effective smoke screen. There would be a small stretch of open space as they left the city proper and crossed to the wood shed and corral, but no one was looking that direction.

People were huddled on the ground as two men strutted circles around them, gesturing and shouting. Each time one of them yelled, the crowd would flinch and huddle closer together. They were traumatized, perfect for spreading exaggerated tales of harsh gods walking the land. Hopefully, my team's actions would dispel a bit of that, though I'm sure none of the villagers would ever forget what they had witnessed that day.

I found my place nestled back in some trees where I could

see the whole village, but no one would be able to see me unless they knew exactly where to look. Aegon, Gracie, and Matt were already in place, crouched behind the low stone wall.

It was the kind of wall you saw everywhere around small villages. They needed to clear rocks off of the land for building or farming, but there was never any good place to put them, so they built walls out of them. Barely waist high and not going anywhere in particular, these walls wandered around the outside of the village, forming a boundary of sorts for the village proper.

I didn't have to wait long. Edana had the farthest to go, so she had been instructed to start as soon as she reached the shed. It was the most dangerous part for her, as her magic was still completely wild.

For that reason, I had insisted that she go inside the woodshed for the maximum effect. I knew her own magic wouldn't hurt her, but the trapped smoke could still burn her lungs. The whole shed could even come down on her. I was depending on Altur to pull her free of whatever came.

The fire came all at once, bursting through every crack of the woodshed, all at once. The villagers screamed and pointed, terrorized by what looked like a new attack. The two sorcerers yelled at them to be quiet, then turned their eyes on the spectacle themselves.

It was an impressive fire, Edana's release of her magic in the dry wooden building had set every part of it on fire simultaneously. I was a little worried that it had worked too well. If the two enemy sorcerers had looked immediately, they might have seen Edana fleeing the building.

As it was, the moment they took to yell at the villagers was enough for the distant figures to dart back behind the other burning buildings and soon I could see Altur and Edana creeping back towards me, holding themselves low to the ground, even though no one could have seen them through the fire and smoke.

The two sorcerers were now talking quietly between themselves. It wouldn't do for the young gods to look confused in front of their hostages, so they separated themselves from the crowd, first yelling at everyone to stay still or they would kill all of the villagers. They whispered to one another, then they both took off walking toward the shed.

I signaled Aegon.

The two took their time investigating the woodshed, walking circuits around it, staring off into the woods, seeing nothing. Their shock came when they turned back to the town to get back to their cowering subjects. Aegon stood in plain sight, leaning up against the low stone wall, smiling as if the whole world were meadows and bluebirds.

Instinctively, the two crouched and spread out, walking slowly towards their old teacher, readying themselves for an attack. They had used a lot of their magic that day, but they still outnumbered him and they had greater control and power over the magic than he did. Even at a distance, I could see cruel smiles on their faces, spiders who had caught a fly.

Aegon laughed as they drew close, a chilling sound, an echo of the madness he had once endured. There was a sick humor in it, a glee that spoke of evil secrets. He was playing his role perfectly and the smiles on the other men's faces faded ever so slightly.

"Tors, Laigo!" Aegon greeted the two by name. "How nice to see me again! I bet you lost a lot of sleep worrying about me, all cold and lost out there in the wilderness. Did you cry? Did you?"

"You know, Humeer wants you for himself," Tors responded. "Said he had all sorts of things planned for you. I don't think he's quite forgiven you for shunning him, you know."

"Well that just breaks my heart, boys. I suppose you want to truss me up and take me back to him, right? What good little dogs you are, playing fetch and everything."

The smiles on the sorcerers' faces grew wider and even crueler. It was clear they had no intention of returning Aegon to Humeer. They knew why he was such a great prize and weren't about to let it slip out of their fingers. They would kill him right here, slowly, if they could manage it.

Aegon saw the truth of it the same as I did. It was what we had expected, after all. In spite of their advances and their clear intentions for violence, he stayed where he was, leaning leisurely against the wall. I knew he would stay that way for the whole battle. If he moved, Matt and Gracie wouldn't be able to reach him anymore. The two of them were still crouched behind the wall, their hands reaching up behind Aegon and resting lightly on his lower back.

It was time for a little theatrics.

"Come to think of it, I never liked you two," Aegon quipped, and let loose with an inferno of fire that slammed into Laigo like a giant fist, knocking him to the ground. It was the kind of thing a sorcerer could do if he released most of his magic, all at one time. From their perspective, it was a showy, stupid thing to do. Laigo was still alive and struggling to his feet and Tors let loose an answering fireball.

This one was small and white hot. The control was amazing, more than I had ever seen, even from Aegon.

Gracie and Matt pulled their hands off of Aegon's back for just a moment as he whispered back to them. I had instructed them to stop feeding him magic when he was being attacked. It was also vital that Aegon be in the middle of a counterattack when their flames hit him.

We had already seen that magic transferred much easier when the user was already using magic. If I was correct, as long as Aegon was using his magic when he was hit, a lot of their magic would be channeled right through him and back at them, minimizing the damage done to Aegon.

It was a matter of intricate timing, but my good soldiers pulled it off without a hitch. When the white ball of flame slammed into Aegon's chest, he was already firing back a thin ribbon of white fire at Tors. The ribbon grew larger and stronger the second that Tors' fireball hit Aegon, the magic flowing through him like a pipe.

Tors had apparently been expecting Aegon to jump away, dodge, or even just die from his attack, so he was caught completely off guard as the counterattack hit him. Aegon looked casual, leaning against the fence, hand raised as if in greeting, pumping flames into the other man.

Gracie and Matt returned their hands to his back, and a small glow spoke to the magic flowing from them into Aegon. With the extra power, Aegon kept up his relentless attack, the ribbon of flame growing as thick as a tree and hot as a sun. Tors only managed the tiniest of yelps before the pillar of flame threw his lifeless body to the ground.

Aegon turned, looking to the stunned and staggering Laigo.

132

The sorcerer who had strutted as a god just minutes before now looked scared. These weren't students any longer, but experts in their magic, and what Aegon had just done was impossible. He had burned through more magic than any one man could muster. He had done it easily, without even standing up, and he looked ready for more.

Laigo looked in panic to his fallen comrade, but the smoke rising from the body told him that Tors would never rise again. Aegon raised his hands, another bright ribbon of flames already dancing between his fingers. Laigo took an involuntary step back, knowing full well he couldn't withstand an attack like the one that had killed Tors.

Aegon paused, visibly considering his options, then waved the flames away.

"Come here," he commanded. Laigo froze, unmoving. Another ribbon of flame leapt from Aegon's hand and struck the other man in the chest, but only for a moment. It wasn't enough to kill him, but it was enough to burn him and break the last of his will. Feeling the incredible heat of the blow coming from someone who should have been bone dry shortly after the first fireball was more than he could process.

"I SAID COME HERE, YOU TRAITOROUS MAGGOT!" Aegon roared, flames licking down both arms. Laigo scurried up to his former teacher.

"Kneel." It was only a whisper, but it carried even more threat now that he stood only an arm's length away. Laigo sunk to his knees in the dust. The twisting of their minds through murder had only made Humeer's followers more afraid of death.

"Are you going to kill me?" Laigo's voice quavered. Aegon

laughed again, taunting his student.

"Of course I'm going to kill you, you slime sucking worm. We both know you deserve it, and we both know I would enjoy it. But first, I need you to carry a message to Humeer. When you're done with that, come back and I'll kill you then, deal?"

"But... umm... I..." Laigo stammered, not sure what he was agreeing to.

"Shut up, shut up, SHUT UP!" Aegon raved, looking every inch the madman. "Does it really look like I need your permission, dog? Don't answer that either, you sniveling kitten. Just go tell Humeer that if he will come to me peacefully, I will grant him a quick death. You got that, little princess?"

Laigo nodded and Aegon put his foot on the kneeling man's chest and kicked hard, sending him sprawling in the dust.

"Then go!" he ordered, sending another small fireball to hurry his messenger on his way. Laigo needed no encouragement and was scrambling away before he even got his feet underneath him to run. The villagers on the ground started to cheer until Aegon silenced them.

"You shut up too, you sheep. There was only two of them and you laid down and sniffed at their boots, crying and whimpering. You just sit right there in the dust until I'm gone, it's where you belong. In fact, don't even look over here. LOOK AWAY!"

The villagers all averted their gaze in an instant, as if strings had been tied to their noses and all pulled at once. They were fairly sure that they had been saved, but nobody was about to anger a monster who was feared even by other monsters.

Matt and Gracie scrambled away, keeping low as best they

could, heading to the rally point back in the trees. Aegon strolled away, providing a point of focus, just in case any of the villagers decided to risk a look. None of them did and soon all of our party was back together under the cover of the neighboring woods.

Chapter 17

A dark man once taught me that balance trumps strength.
When a man is off balance, a feather is enough to knock him
over.

–Musings of the Historian

"We did it!" exulted Altur, the simple farmer was glowing
with the success of our endeavor. All he saw was that we had saved
the village and Edana was fine, that was all that mattered to him. He
didn't understand why the rest of the faces in the group were
solemn.

"Ah hope you got somethin' amazin' planned next, Tory,"
drawled Matt. "We just threw all in."

"Anybody got anything left? Edana? Aegon?" Gracie did a
quick inventory around the group, but everyone was shaking their
heads. "Me neither. I hate to agree with my brother, Tory, but this
plan of yours has put us in an awfully vulnerable position. I don't see
how this makes anything better."

"What are you all talking about?" Altur was completely lost.
"We just saved all these people and made the evil sorcerers look like
fools. We even killed one of them, now they're down to thirteen, why
is everyone so upset about this?"

"You see..." Gracie started to respond in a patient tone, but

Aegon interrupted.

"You're as blind as you are stupid, farmer. These two had no packs, not even so much as a canteen of water. Naturally they wouldn't if they wanted to pull off the whole gods routine. That means that wherever they came from, it's not that far away, likely less than a few hours' march."

"I don't understand why..." Altur started to defend himself, but Aegon ripped into him again, taking his anger out on the poor farmer.

"That's just it! You don't understand! Every magic user in this camp is bone dry. If we combined everything we had, we could barely light a candle. It will be days before we could actually fight. Meanwhile, we just sent a survivor off to Humeer with a message sure to bring all of them in force. They might be back through here by nightfall. We didn't save a village, we threw the doors open for a massacre and our heads are first on the block!"

"If that's true, then why did we let him go?" Altur wondered. "I know I don't understand the magic, but it seemed like you could have finished him easily."

"Of course I could have! I didn't even need magic, I could have used my knife as he knelt before me. That's what we should have done. Then we would have had days, maybe even a week to recharge before Humeer figured out his advance party wasn't advancing."

"So why didn't you?"

"Because HE told me not to!" Aegon shouted back, flinging an accusing finger at me, though he winced at the sudden movement. The fireball he had taken to the chest had not all been redirected and he was badly injured.

"He's the Master, the Historian, who's supposed to lead us to a surprising victory against impossible odds. Well I can tell you one thing, it's going to be surprising indeed if he plans to pull it off using only moronic decisions."

He finished his rant and set to fuming and pouting, likely thinking up new insults for his next tirade. Gracie laid a hand on my arm.

"I don't doubt you, I really don't, but I also don't understand why you didn't let us finish Laigo. It would have made things much better for us."

"Anyone else want to lead?" I offered. My voice was quiet, but everyone could hear the challenge in my tone. Heads dropped or shook ever so slightly.

They had seen the enemy today. The enemy sorcerers were shockingly powerful. If our timing had even been more than a second off today, they likely would have all been killed by just the two sorcerers. Now they were going to be facing thirteen, possibly all at once, and I was the only one who didn't look afraid.

"We're not saying that, Tory," Gracie reassured me as Aegon scoffed behind her. "You're in command and we'll obey you, as we promised. Perhaps this would be simpler if you told us what we're supposed to do next."

"We attack," I replied, and I couldn't help but smile at the looks of disbelief on their faces. "We have the advantage at this moment. We need to strike again to level the playing field and keep them off balance."

"What in the muck stink of all pig slop are you talking

138

about?" Aegon gasped. "How are we supposed to attack? It would be suicide! We are weak!"

"That is why we must make it look like we are stronger than ever," I argued back. "They know that they are more powerful, they know that their magic is stronger, and they know that they outnumber us. If we attack now, right now, they might not know all those things anymore."

"Count me in!" Matt was smiling too by now. "Ah have no idea what you got in your head, but t'way Ah see it, we was dead when we started. Iffn' you think you can do what you just said, Ah want t'be there t'see it."

"He's certainly right about the 'dead' part," Aegon grumbled. "I guess we've got to see this through."

"Great, take a second to eat something, rest. Aegon and I need to have a little chat."

"If you..." Aegon started to protest, but I grabbed him by the arm and escorted him away from the group forcefully. The decisions I had made in the last twelve hours had been brutal on me, a physical pain like I had never felt was building in my head. I intended to have my wage. I let him go as soon as we were out of earshot of the others, who were already sitting on the ground, exhausted from their forced march.

"I just handed you a victory, tell me how your Historian stopped being a Historian."

Aegon scowled at me, but he replied.

"He remembered his name."

"His name? His true name?"

"Oh yes. He remembered his name and everything that came

before. It all crashed into his mind at once."

"And?"

"What do you mean, 'and?'"

"And what happened to him when he remembered?"

"I'll tell you this," he sneered. "He barely survived it."

"Explain yourself, please," I pleaded with him, but to no avail.

"Forget it, that's all you get for this 'victory' that's left us helpless. I can only hope we don't have too many more such victories under your command. We may win ourselves to death."

He brushed me to the side and stalked back to the others, settling down on the ground by the packs and shoving a fistful of bread into his mouth. I had hoped to get more from him. He had certainly left more questions than answers. He had still given me a lot, though I'm sure he didn't mean to.

I had learned that I did have a name, I just didn't know it. I also knew now that there was an end to it all, there was some point where I would remember everything, apparently all at once. I brushed easily enough past his taunt that the process had nearly killed the other Historian.

I knew he meant it to worry me, but it was more than I could have asked for to know that he had actually survived it. In my heart, I had always suspected that the only end there could be would be death, if it ever came at all. His taunt had been a bonus, a promise of a greater adventure, one that was truly my own.

I let them rest only half an hour before I gave the command to pack up to start walking. I noticed that Aegon had trouble rising and I took a closer look. He had come out of the battle worse than I had originally thought. He had been able to re-channel a lot of heat

140

from the fireball Tors had launched at him, but not all. A patch of ugly scorched flesh nestled on his ribs, almost under his arm.

His tolerance for pain was admirable. He hadn't even healed from the burns he sustained while saving Edana. Then his back had been burned repeatedly during our experiments with the magic. The burn on his ribs was the worst of them, by far, and it was starting to wear him down.

He had been running on adrenaline just after the battle, but now the wound was stiffening up. There was nothing I could do for it, and he didn't complain, so we started walking. It slowed him down and I saw him wince a time or two when he tripped on rocks. The others noticed as well, but after he spent a full minute cursing at Gracie for offering to help, they left him alone.

I led the way, tracking the fleeing sorcerer. Laigo was no kind of woodsman and he left generous tracks. Even when his path went over rocks and hard packed ground, he still broke branches and bent over weeds to mark his path. Thanks to his carelessness, we were able to keep up a pretty good pace in our pursuit. I wanted to strike while the confusion was still fresh in their minds.

Near the end of his path, Laigo must have realized how easily he could be followed and started taking measures he must have thought were clever. When he crossed a small stream, he walked in the water for a while to disguise his tracks. For reasons I never have quite understood, men will almost always walk upstream when using this tactic. I gambled on this and led the company towards the mountains, following the stream.

Sure enough, after only a hundred yards or so, I spotted his muddy footprints leaving the stream. His cleverness had cost him. Now he also had wet shoes and pants, adding water drips and mud to his trail.

The rest of the party was quite impressed with my tracking skill, not understanding how easy it had been. As four out of the five were farmers, they hadn't much experience in tracking anything cleverer than a cow through the woods. Even Aegon, who had spent a lot of his time in the wilderness, had been insane most of the time, and had never become a true woodsman.

At one juncture, Laigo tried to be clever again and walked backwards, trying to suggest a different direction. The tiny scuffs in the dirt behind his heels showed his deceit as clear as day. Really, tracking at that point was almost meaningless, I could already smells traces of wood smoke in the air. If we went too much further, we would stumble right into their camp, I whispered for everyone to stop and motioned them to circle up around me.

"For this attack, I need Aegon, Altur, and Gracie." I conducted the whole briefing at a whisper, just in case there were any guards posted. I shouldn't have worried, they didn't think they had anything to fear in this world.

"Aegon, Matt, I need you to channel any shreds of magic you might have into Gracie."

"I'm not going to be able to fight," she warned me. "Even with everything we have left, I won't be able to do much more than a puff."

"That's all I need," I assured her. Luckily, Gracie was wearing a farmer's shirt and trousers, not a dress like Edana. She was able to lift the back of her shirt to give access to Aegon and Matt, who transferred any magic they might have charged up in the couple hours we had been walking. The handprints on Gracie's back might as well have been caused by two slaps, the amount of magic too

142

miniscule to burn.

"Edana, Matt, I need the two of you to find us a campsite. We need somewhere hidden, but with a good field of view. Make sure there are at least three ways out, no caves. No fires either. Go now."

I knew Matt especially wanted to stay and watch, but they slipped away without arguing. I turned back to my three remaining soldiers.

"Aegon, your role here is just to be seen, and just once. I need for them to see you unharmed."

"But I am bloody well harmed!" He hissed back at me. He pointed to where a few drops of blood seeped from the charred wound.

"I know that, and they will suspect it after they've heard the story. They might think it best to come in force to hunt you down while you're still weak. We need to show them that's a bad idea. You need to at least act unhurt for about five seconds."

"Then what? They'll just run me down and slaughter me. I can barely walk, you expect me to run?"

"No, I expect Altur to carry you."

"You've got to be out of your greasy feather brain! I'm not about to let someone carry me!"

"Then run," I shrugged, he blanched a little at the thought. I had bigger things on my mind than his pride. The interfering had only been getting harder on me, and this would be my biggest transgression of all. I would directly participate, the gloves were off.

"Altur, as soon as Aegon is seen by everyone and ducks back into cover, you pick him up and run like the very devil. If you can find the others, great. If not, meet back here and we'll all go together."

He nodded his understanding, ready to go in spite of his exhausting day. My respect for that lumbering tragic farmer rose a little more.

"Gracie, I need you to be my shadow. They need to see me, but not you. Our job will be to find a spot where you can be behind me, but not be seen. Aegon, I'll need an introduction."

A thin smile worked its way onto his pained face. He was beginning to understand.

We crept in together until we could see the camp itself, then split up, Altur with Aegon, Gracie with me.

Men dressed in the rough leathers of Aegon's school sat in tight circles around the camp, talking in hushed tones. Slaves scurried about the camp, packing things up and taking tents down.

It was as I had expected, they had decided to go hunting for Aegon, all of them. We had come just in time. All thirteen of them would mow through the land like a plague, destroying everything in their path to find Aegon before his powers charged to full.

Aegon had been instructed to wait for a while once he was in position to give us time to find our own spot, but I didn't trust his patience. Gracie followed close behind me as I circled the camp, finally finding what I was looking for, a large tree with a large shrub growing at the base. We ducked behind the tree and I whispered my final instructions to Gracie. When she understood, I peeked around the bottom of the shrub to watch the camp. I didn't have to wait long.

"Oh Humee-eer!" Aegon sang out like a mother calling her child in from play. His voice had the effect of a whiplash on the camp, all eyes snapping to where he leaned up against a tree, calm and smiling. His arms were folded across his chest, hiding the burn mark on his clothes. "Where are you, you psycho butcher?"

A man with thick blond hair burst out of the largest of the tents, one of the only ones still standing. He stared in disbelief at his old teacher.

"Just wanted you to know there was no ill will." Aegon took full advantage of their stunned immobility. They weren't sure if he was going to strike and everyone looked ready to dodge more than attack. "I'm going to kill you, of course, but I wanted you to know it wasn't because I was angry or anything. You see, I have new students now. I think it's time you met one of them."

He slipped behind the tree, out of view and the sound of running steps was heard retreating through the woods. Humeer turned on Laigo, who stood close by.

"You told me he was hurt!"

"He was... he uh... Tors' fireball would have punched through a..." Laigo's stammering reply was cut short as Humeer knocked him to the ground with a vicious backhand. He started ordering the other men around, arranging a pursuit.

It was show time. Fighting down a sick, tortured feeling, I stepped into full view of the camp, head down. I felt Gracie step up behind me, matching my stance and pressing herself against my back. I felt her small hand slide into mine, still out of view, awaiting my signal.

The camp must have been in a lot of turmoil indeed, because it took almost a full minute before anyone noticed me, standing like a specter at the edge of camp.

"Who's that?"

That was my cue. I raised my head to look at them, squeezing Gracie's hand at the same time. Her control was superb and she used the little breath of magic she had to send threads of fire twisting around my arms, along with a fiery aura that flared for just a moment all around me. The magic spent, she ducked back behind the tree, the shrub covering her retreat.

While Aegon's appearance had stunned them into inaction, my appearance and the promise of magic had the opposite effect.

Almost in unison, thirteen hands raised and spouted fire at me. I dived to the side, rolling away and dodging their attacks. This only made them more desperate. More fireballs, ribbons of flame, and walls of heat chased after me as I ducked, ran and rolled away from them all.

As a Historian, I could move very quickly when I needed to, a useful skill when one needed to check in on a distant part of a story. While my mind writhed and rebelled at using this power in front of witnesses, it was amazingly effective. To them I appeared inhuman, skittering away from their flames faster than any mortal could move.

It would appear as magic, new magic. Their attacks grew more frantic, it was time to drive it home.

I stopped suddenly, standing up, almost in the middle of them, smiling a truly evil smile. All thirteen unleashed all the magic they had left, using their superior control to focus it into a barrage of white hot beams. I was reminded of the lasers I had seen on other worlds, beams of energy capable of cutting through any material with ease. These flames they threw at me now were like that, their ability to focus the fire was superhuman. It was the power of emotions made real, put in the hands of psychopaths.

As I felt the bands of flame tear at me, I threw back my head and laughed, deep and throaty. It was a wrenching sound. I focused the agony I felt in my own head and channeled it into the laugh, filling it with cruelty and sick amusement. The flames focused even more as panic fueled their mania.

All at once, their magic ran out. I brought my head back down to look at them, each one in his turn, pausing a moment longer to let my eyes linger on Humeer. One of them tried to take a step back when my eyes fell on him. His heel caught on a root and he tripped, landing hard in the dirt.

I laughed again and raised my hand as if to attack. They all flinched backwards, even the one on the ground. I laughed harder.

"Don't worry, little children, Aegon has something special in mind for you."

I turned and walked out of the clearing, slowly. They would panic now. Their fire had done nothing to me. They would connect that with what they had just seen from Aegon. They would believe that he wasn't hurt because their magic had no effect on him anymore.

Their doubts had become fears and their fears would become panic by the time morning came. A night spent lying awake wondering what Aegon would do to them would do quite a number on their psyche. Desperation would do more than we ever could.

Chapter 18

It tortures the mind, knowing that you don't know enough when it truly matters.
    –Musings of the Historian

Gracie and I tracked the group back to the new camp where Matt and Edana had already set up a meal. Aegon and Altur were already there, helping. Everything stopped abruptly and they gathered around when we came into camp. Their eyes widened further and further as Gracie described what had happened in vivid detail.

"Oh, how I wish I could have seen that." Aegon was giddy, rubbing his hands together like a miser. "Humeer's got to be going nuts. He's never been able to handle not understanding something, it's what made him so successful as a sorcerer."

"That's the plan," I concurred. Aegon was giddy, like a child with a puppy. Already I had plans to pull him to the side and ask more questions after diner, strike while the iron was hot.

"So what will they do now? Will they come hunting for us?" The question came from Edana.

"No," I assured her. "We've bought ourselves some time. Tonight they will scramble, worried about an attack. They used up practically all of their magic trying to kill me.

"We'll lose some ground when the attack doesn't come, they'll start to wonder if our magic has some limitations after all."

"Why can't we attack again, like we did tonight?" Altur asked, ever the straightforward man.

"I can't do that again," I replied, my voice breaking. It was almost a sob, though I fought to maintain control. Once again, every eye was on me, concerned this time. I couldn't make them understand, but it was true, my ability to participate was diminishing.

It was getting worse by the hour. Direct participation in this story was making it my own when it wasn't. I don't know how to explain the feeling, any more that Aegon could describe the emotion that governed his magic. All I can say is that it felt deeply unnatural. My very soul was sickened by it.

Worst of all, the effect was cumulative. Each time I acted, it made me feel a little sicker and it didn't fade. I now struggled under the combined weight of all my decisions in this story, I could hardly think straight. I knew it wouldn't leave until I walked away from this story and the horizons shifted.

They gathered around me then. They didn't understand what I was going through, but they understood that it hurt. My eyes stung as Gracie laid her hand on my arm and told me that it was going to be all right. Altur stepped forward and put his arms around me in a bear hug.

"Tory, you're my best friend, and you have done more for us than we could have prayed for. We would never ask you to do something if it's going to take that much from you."

"I might," quipped Aegon, but his heart wasn't in it and it

came across as a joke. Edana and Matt took their turns expressing their thanks and support in turn. The whole time, Gracie's hand never left my arm. It became the default position for her whenever we were together. There was never anything more, just the touch of human warmth to comfort me.

"You know, you could tell us whatcha need done next, let us do a touch a' this, how 'bout?" Matt offered. I latched on, focusing on the story.

"Right now, we need to rest. The magic users need to store up their magic. They will panic now, and that gains us some time. I made sure they drained their magic as well, so we've leveled the playing field."

"Oh yes, thirteen masters against our six rejects. Sounds like a fair fight, all right," Aegon mocked out of instinct, but it still lacked any bite.

"We've got a Historian," Gracie pointed out, giving my arm a squeeze. "I think we should give them a chance to surrender."

Everyone chuckled at the thought. I continued to lay out the situation. My tone was serious and low as I tried to focus through the internal chaos.

"It gets tricky now. They're unstable, which makes them even more dangerous. They might even start to turn on each other, they've already reaped benefits from betrayal. I'd bet anything that some of them have already considered it. That would be a benefit for us, but we need Humeer to stay in command, at least for a while longer."

"I trust you, Tory," Altur reassured, "but isn't he the smartest and the most powerful of them all? Seems like we'd have an easier time of it if we could get shut of the wolf and just deal with the dogs."

"That time will come, but we can't leave anything to chance. If Humeer dies, then they scatter and wreak havoc through the whole valley, twelve armies instead of one. Worse, someone else might take command, someone stupid."

"Wouldn't that be a good thing?" Edana suggested.

"Quite the opposite. Smart people always make smart decisions, and I can predict what those decisions will be. Stupid people, however, are limitless in their stupidity, doubly so when they're afraid. They could do anything at all. If we have to wait to react to their decisions, we'll be too slow, be caught out of position, and slaughtered to the man."

"Got it, you need a genius leading them so you can know what they're going to do," Altur summed up.

"Not a genius," I corrected. "A genius is far too close to a stupid person, unpredictable. Humeer isn't a genius, only very smart and endlessly curious."

"What's the difference? Isn't a genius just a very smart person?"

I shook my head.

"The intelligence is similar, but a smart person is a campfire, bright and useful. A genius is a bonfire, powerful, unstable, and destructive, even to themselves."

"Which might you be?" Matt asked softly.

"That's enough!" Aegon came to my rescue unexpectedly, his expression a frozen mask. He was serious again. He had found the discussion as disturbing as I did. "As much as I'm enjoying all this gossip and hand holding, I'd like it even more if you would all shut your drooling faces. Historian, the lesson's over. What are they going to do next and what do you want us to do about it?"

"Humeer will move the group. He is facing an unknown force of unknown power. He will get to a position of strength, some place he can defend easily and see us coming. Once they're feeling safe again, he'll send out scouts to gather information, try to learn our weaknesses and location."

"Makes sense, go on."

"We need to make sure Humeer makes it to that spot alive. We need to set up a watch, make sure he isn't surprised in his sleep before they make it to whatever stronghold they choose."

"We need to guard Humeer?" Edana was incredulous, but she didn't argue against it.

"Once they're in their stronghold, we can keep them bottled up there, keep them off balance. That would be a good time to kill Humeer, if we can. In short, we want perfect order until they make it to where we can keep an eye on them, then we want all the panic and disorder we can stir up."

Matt laughed out loud, slapping his knee.

"That's prime, Tory. Ah nevah could have thought a' somethin' like that. Almost makes a body wonder if we might just win this thing. A squirrel treein' a hound. Ah'll take first watch, don't want nothin' t' happen to our golden boy."

Still chuckling to himself, he scooped up some bread and a water sack to head back out to the woods.

"Above all," I warned. "You can't let yourself be seen. We've built this war on smoke. If they see flesh and blood behind it, we're lost, all of us. If you see some sign of treachery, throw a rock at the tent and clear out. Humeer is no fool, he'll be expecting it as well. All we need to do is give him an extra edge."

"It's done, Tory." He nodded and slipped away.

"I'll take next," volunteered Gracie. I nodded.

"It's going to be delicate work. We'll have to keep up with them, monitor them, but without ever betraying our own presence. A slip here will destroy everything, I don't think I could repair it now."

With the plan all laid out, I turned to Aegon, opening my mouth to invite him to speak privately. Edana beat me to the punch.

"Tory, could I talk with you a moment, alone?" Aegon grinned at me, knowing I had been thwarted. I couldn't think of any reason not to, so I nodded and followed her away from the group. We were well out of hearing range before she turned on me.

"Altur loves me," she blurted out. "That's why he stayed when my father died. That's why he stayed when the madness took me. I'm right, aren't I?"

I couldn't help but smile. We had just endured a full day of fire and death, but she hadn't been able to move past our last conversation back at the farmhouse.

"Yes, that's right. So what?" I taunted. "You obviously don't feel the same way about him, he's just a farm hand."

It may have been a little mean of me, but I was feeling mean at the moment. There was too much weighing on my mind and soul to play the role of her girlfriend. She stamped her foot in frustration.

"I never... I'm not like..." Her anger built with each failed defense. "I don't know, all right? I get that you know everything all the time, but the rest of us mortals have to figure these things out one step at a time."

"So you're saying you might love him back?" It wasn't subtle, but I was beyond a gentle touch by that point.

"I don't know," she admitted. If the moon had been a bit brighter, I imagined I might have seen a bit of a blush. "I never saw him like that. I always knew he was a good man, I just haven't seen him as a..." She struggled to find a word.

"Man?" I offered. She nodded in the darkness. "You'd be surprised how many wives have the same problem with their husbands. Don't worry, you'll figure it out, you have the time. Altur isn't going anywhere."

She nodded again.

"Would you mind going back to the camp without me?" she asked, her voice soft and emotional. "I need a moment to myself."

"Of course." The truth was, I was anxious to get away. Aegon saw me coming and nodded, rising to his feet and heading into the woods in the opposite direction Edana and I had gone. I caught up to him and we walked a while in the darkness. There must have been a lot weighing on his mind to distract him from the pain at his side. We walked several minutes in the darkness before he finally stopped.

"Ask your question, Historian, you earned it."

"You've mentioned that there is someone or something controlling me. Did the other Historian remember what it was?"

"Yes, he remembered them, though it was a little strange to hear his description."

"Them?"

"He said it was a small group of people. He said he met them outside of time. I'm not sure how that's possible. Do you have any idea what he might have meant?"

"No idea," I admitted. Time was a fuzzy concept for someone like me, it always seemed to shift when the horizons did, but I couldn't imagine something happening outside of time entirely.

"Shame. He said that they could control reality itself, something to do with their souls."

"Souls?"

"Are all of your questions going to be repeats of what I've already said? Yes, their souls. He said they were different somehow. He said it was like a tree growing in a river. The birds know the air and nothing else, the fish know the water, and the grubs know the mud underneath it all. The people who did this to you are the tree, in all the places at once."

"Amazing," I gasped. "Power like that would make them gods."

"The thought crossed my mind, but he said that they weren't. They said that there was something above them, a power they could only sense, but never touch."

"Why?"

"How would I know something like that, you ancient clod? I don't even understand what I just told you."

"Sorry, I was distracted. The question I meant to ask was: why did they make him a Historian? Why did they do this to me?"

"No." He shook his head wildly, backing away a step. "That's enough for tonight."

"What will I have to do to hear that from you, Aegon? I've done plenty already, and I can barely stand it, you owe me!"

"That may be," he admitted. "But it's the last thing I know, and once you hear it, you won't stay."

"I promise I will!" I pleaded.

"I promise you won't. I know you've paid your dues, but I need you to finish this, to erase my sin. I can't let you know the truth until this is done. For what it's worth, I am sorry."

I raged inside, but there was nothing I could do. I knew I couldn't force the information from him, my hands were tied. I had to continue this nightmare to its bitter end. I stomped away from him, leaving him in the dark and returning to camp, plopping down on a log to fume and focus on something besides the growing sickness inside me. That is how the night passed.

I barely noticed Gracie's hand on my arm.

Chapter 19

Faith is courage.

–Musings of the Historian

The night passed, the members of the group taking turns watching over Humeer. There was treachery on the first night as Matt noticed a shadow moving towards the big tent. He threw a pebble at the side of the tent that barely made a sound in the still night, but it was enough. There was a slight whisper of movement inside the tent. The shadow must have heard it too, because it faded back into the night, abandoning any ideas of assassination.

The slaves they had brought with them weren't so lucky. The sorcerers forced them to finish packing up the camp that very night. When it was done, daggers appeared suddenly and the slaves were killed. Whether they did it to conserve resources or if they were trying to strengthen their magic even more, I didn't know.

For the next couple days, our group acted like shepherds, following close behind our powerful prey, but never so close as to spook them into foolishness. It didn't take long to discern their destination. They were headed to the mountains. The closer we got, the darker Aegon's expression became.

"Do you know where we are?" I asked him. He nodded.

"We'll have to stop soon," he informed me. "As soon as they reach the cave, they'll have a line of sight over this whole valley. We need to find a place we can stay hidden."

"Cave? There's a cave near here?"

He nodded, looking a little sick.

"The cave... my cave." Understanding dawned. We were heading to the cave Aegon had lived in when he had discovered the magic. "It's big enough for all of them. From there, they can see for miles around them, it's one of the things I loved about it, even as a lunatic. They wouldn't even need their magic to defend themselves there, they could just as easily roll boulders down on our heads."

I let it all soak in. True to form, Humeer had found them a perfect fortress. It was the high ground in every sense. It even had the added benefit of making Aegon uncomfortable. His memories of this place would bring back the agony and trauma he had endured as the madness had burned away pieces of his tortured mind.

I had to come up with a plan, and soon. My options were fading quickly. The torment I was enduring because of my interference was making it hard to think clearly. My memory was unresponsive as I tried to call up images of situations like this. I knew that I had witnessed battles like this before, an inferior force defeating an entrenched enemy, but I couldn't remember them anymore. It was like my mind was breaking down, a natural safety set in place to stop exactly what I was attempting.

I called the others over to me and explained what was happening. Every face was solemn as they absorbed this new bit of bad news.

"I suspected that we would get to this point," Aegon admitted. "I had hoped we would be a little further along when it happened, though. Are you still able to continue?"

I shrugged.

"It's hard to say. I'll stay to the end, that shouldn't be a problem, but I don't think I can interfere much more. I'll try to think of some sort of strategy for this immediate problem, but I don't think I'll be able to plan much more after that, certainly not participate in any way."

"But you will stay?" Gracie asked the question and even in my beleaguered state, I could hear the undertones behind the question.

"I will stay until the story is done," I confirmed, promising nothing. Still, she looked relieved and that made me feel happy, at least for a moment.

"Let's set up camp, we can see them well enough from here once they start up the mountain to the cave. We may not be able to sneak up on them, but they won't be able to move without us seeing them, either."

Surprisingly, it was Altur who took the lead, not because of any particular leadership abilities or ambitions, but because he understood that making more decisions would hurt his friend, Tory.

I was grateful to sit on a rock, watching them. It felt right to sit and watch as other people interacted and conversed, making decisions about tents and food. At one point, there was some discussion about whether or not they should build a fire. A few of them snuck glances at me, wondering if it was a big enough decision to warrant disturbing my watchful meditation.

Aegon stepped in this time and made the call, telling them to build two fires. One small fire would be hidden, a classic cook fire for roasting food and boiling water. The other would be a large fire, clearly visible from the cave. He reasoned that I had already said that we needed Humeer and his minions bottled up in the cave, so it was likely better for them to think that their enemies were at the gates. It was good logic, the decision I would have made, and it made me smile that someone else had made it.

The danger to them now (I already started to think of the party as "them," rather than "us.") was Humeer starting to branch out, trying to gather information on this new threat. Humeer was smart enough to figure it out, eventually. The little party needed to make sure the mystery stayed front and center in their minds.

In that moment, it became "us" again and I had a flash of a plan. Fighting the discomfort, I called Aegon over to me and whispered my plan in his ear. He started to ask a clarifying question, but the pained look on my face shut him up. He nodded and went to work.

Once the camp was set up and the two fires built, he sent Gracie to watch over the larger fire, making sure it had plenty of fuel to last the night. He warned her about not being seen. If Humeer did have a moment of boldness, or just didn't care if one of his own men died, he might send a scout down to check out the fire. It was important that they find it abandoned, burning on its own.

He then sent Altur and Matt out into the forest to look for young trees that could be chopped down and used for poles. When they were gone, he rooted through the packs and handed one of the extra blankets to Edana, along with a knife, drawing in the dirt what he wanted her to do.

All the while, I sat and watched. I had made a wild gamble. I could hardly trust my own mind and as I considered what was going to happen, I knew that there was a lot that could go wrong. There

160

was nothing I could do about it, though. My time of interfering was over, I knew that now. I had barely been able to voice the words to Aegon, detailing my scheme.

I would finish this story as a Historian, a detached witness. It wasn't a choice anymore, but an overpowering compulsion. I even considered leaving early, seeking some relief by walking on to whatever came next. I found that I couldn't even do that anymore. My course was set. There was a story here and I would witness it to the end.

I called Aegon over and he came at a jog, anxious for some new tidbit of information. His countenance fell when he heard what I had to say.

"You're on your own."

"You're sure?"

"Completely. I will watch, but I can't be a part of this any longer. I hope that you will live up to your end of the bargain. I don't think I can even ask anymore, or attempt to influence you in any way."

"Wow, you must be hard up. I never thought I'd feel sorry for a Historian, but you look pathetic."

"I believe you. Your sympathy is most stirring," I grumbled. He grinned again and wandered back to where Edana was busy cutting the blanket into triangles.

Every once in a while, Altur and Matt would stagger back into camp, dragging some tree behind them. They would drop it by the fire and head back out into the woods. The sun was already behind the mountain when they finally brought in their last one, five in all.

Still they worked, by the light of the cook fire, using their knives and a hatchet to trim the branches away from the trunks and strip off the bark. Slowly but surely, five poles took form, white and slender. As they finished one, Edana would step in, tying one of her flags to the thin end of the pole. Aegon fussed and fluttered around them like a watchful butterfly, anxious that everything be exactly right.

When the poles were done and the cloth flags fixed to the tops, Aegon helped gather all of them into a bundle and the three men took off into the night. It was the one advantage the group had in the night. Aegon had spent years in this territory and knew the lay of the land like a man would know his own home. I followed them, a dutiful observer.

They finally arrived in the open spot at the base of the mountain. The woods fell away here and formed an open field just below the cave. It wouldn't be in striking range of magic or boulders, so it was safe enough, but it would be in plain view of the cave above.

The men worked quickly and quietly, talking in whispers and only when absolutely necessary. Working under the cover of night, they soon had all five poles erect, the flags on top shifting only slightly under the night breeze.

Back at the fire, they warmed themselves and congratulated each other. Edana had already gone to sleep for the night. Matt asked Aegon what the point of all of it was, but Aegon only shrugged and explained that I had told him to and that was all he knew. Matt turned to where I was sitting on my log and started to walk over. Aegon caught him by the arm and shook his head.

"He can't help us anymore, so don't bother."

Matt still stared after me a minute longer, concern and curiosity battling on his face, but he finally turned back to the fire and shared a joke with Altur. Before long, Matt went out to the bonfire to relieve Gracie. Altur promised to take the next shift and turned into bed.

When Gracie came back into camp, only Aegon and I were awake. She went straight to Aegon and spoke quietly with him for a minute before coming over and sitting next to me on the log. Her hand took up its customary station on my arm in her quiet expression of support and comfort.

"Why isn't Aegon sleeping?" she mused aloud. "I would have thought he'd be exhausted. Morning will be here soon."

"His mind is on the day to come. He's worried that if he falls asleep, he'll miss his moment in the morning. He'll need to be by the flags when the first of the other sorcerers wakes up."

It didn't hurt to share my observations about others, as long as I didn't influence anything. She was kind enough not to ask any questions about the plan, but accepted my cool analysis at face value.

"So why don't you sleep? Aegon has already told me that you can't be a part of it anymore."

"I don't sleep," I admitted. "I don't get tired."

"But if you don't sleep, how do you dream?" Her question was playful. She wasn't really searching for any information, she was only trying to distract me from my own mental pain, sacrificing her own night's sleep by doing so.

"I do dream, after a fashion." It felt good to talk, so I talked, enjoying my attentive audience. "When I'm out walking, there comes a time when the horizons shift. It's hard to describe it. It's not like I travel or move, my footsteps don't even break rhythm, but somehow the worlds change and I'm in a new place.

"Whenever that happens, I get flashes. Nothing you could put together into a full thought. It's a mix of random images, sounds, and feelings. They don't match anything I remember from my travels, so I think they are from my life before, something that leaks through during the shift."

"What sort of things have you seen?"

"Nothing I could describe as a full scene, just bits. I have definitely seen stone, rough and grey, with my hand on it. It's one thing that has come through several times. I've wondered, when I'm wandering empty worlds, if I could have been a stone cutter. I think I would have liked that sort of thing."

"Really?" she laughed lightly. "It seems like rough work for a storyteller. Why would you like it?"

"It lasts. I've wandered over so many ruins and wondered about the stories of the people who had lived there. One thing that impresses me is that the stones outlast everything. Wood rots, metal rusts, concrete cracks, and wind and rain wash it all away. Even after the buildings have all fallen to dust, the stones still bear the marks of the stonecutter, echoes of his hands."

"I guess I never thought of it that way. Have you ever tried to settle down? You wouldn't have to be a part of other people's stories, you could just sit and watch the world, let the stories come to you."

"I've never tried. I've always felt the desire to walk. I've done a kind of settling down before. I've waited decades in one place to see how some story ended, though that doesn't happen very often. But even in all that time, the place never starts to feel like home. If anything, the longer I stay in a place, the more I want to leave."

"How do you know when a story is finished? It seems like you would have to stay by someone their whole life to truly see their story through to the end."

"I just know," I shrugged. "It comes all at once, usually right after some big event. The desire to walk on becomes overwhelming. I've never tried to fight it. When it comes, there's nothing I want more than new ground under my feet."

She rose then, crossing to the packs to pull out a couple blankets. She draped one over my shoulders, then spun the other one around behind herself, letting it settle around her. She took her seat again, her hand settling on my arm in the same motion. She had run out of questions, or maybe her mind was still on my answers. In any case, neither of us spoke again until the horizon behind us started to glow faintly, a promise of a new sunrise.

Chapter 20

It is one of man's greatest perversions that, in his pursuit of comfort, he divorces himself from nature.
–Musings of the Historian

Aegon took off through the brush to take up his station at the flags. The others had all been instructed to stay behind, but I was not one of them. I moved quickly, walking a wide arc around Aegon, coming out of the woods where they ran up against the mountains. A ways up the hillside, I could see an outcropping of rock. I picked my way up the mountain, careful not to disturb any dirt or rocks that would cascade and betray my presence.

Once at the outcropping, I could see everything. Aegon stood like a statue by the poles. A morning wind whipped the flags fitfully, but the poles had been set solidly into the ground during the night. To my right, I could just see the entrance to the cave. There was a bit of packed earth right in front of the cave that made for a sort of front porch. Once the sun finally poked its head above the tree line, washing the mountain in brightness, a shuffling step brought one of the sorcerers to the mouth of the cave.

He stretched and yawned, scratching at his stomach as he made the weary transition into full consciousness. Wakefulness came to him abruptly as his eyes fell on Aegon, standing alone in the valley. The sun at his back, Aegon's face was still in shadow, but there could be no mistaking who it was. The man dived back into the cave, shouting an alarm to the others.

Like a kicked anthill, the cave mouth was soon alive with people. I got my first really good look at them as they all clustered together, looking to the man below. Three of them were women, though I would have to change my definition to call them feminine. Their look was as savage as the men.

Humeer was immediately recognizable. His intelligent eyes were a deep blue, his sandy brows pulled together in a look of deep concern.

"What do you want?" he yelled down the mountain. His voice carried easily in the crisp morning air. Aegon continued to stand motionless for another couple minutes. His talent for theatrics had grown considerably while under my command.

He realized now that what people saw wasn't nearly as important as what they thought they saw. It was a subtle difference, but it made all the difference in the world. This plan would fall apart if they saw him as one man standing by some poles. They needed to see an enigma, a promise of faceless destruction.

When he finally moved, he didn't say a word. He reached a hand out and wrapped it around the pole nearest to him. All at once, fiery threads wrapped around the entire length of the pole, setting it on fire at all parts at once. The flag was gone in seconds. The wood was green and smoked furiously, fighting the flames. He poured more magic into it, hearing the sap pop and crackle as the wood charred under his touch.

When it was burnt enough, he toppled it. He raised his arm again to point at the remaining four poles. His wrist and finger were bent, ever so slightly, giving it the impression of a skeletal claw. He held the pose for a full minute before he turned and disappeared again into the woods.

I felt a sliver of pride at his performance. I hadn't been able to describe how it needed to be done, I had only given him the sequence. It turned out that the teacher made for an excellent student and he had filled in the blanks on his own. He had even used far more magic than he needed to in burning the pole. Every sorcerer in the cave would have recognized the complete disregard for their power.

It was a bold statement for a single person to stand against thirteen, then blatantly run his own magic down. It would reinforce in their minds that he had leap-frogged them in their understanding of the magic. He had openly flaunted the fact that he could throw his magic around with impunity and still have plenty left over to deal with them.

It wasn't true, of course. It was altogether likely that Aegon was back in camp right this moment, enduring the burns it took to have Matt and Gracie recharge his magic with their own. It wouldn't be much, of course, it had only taken a couple days for the party to reach the caves, not enough for any of them to recharge fully. It was a dangerous time. Any attack would be a slaughter.

Luckily, an attack was the furthest thing from Humeer's mind at that moment. I could hear loud arguing coming from the cave and circled around, heading up the mountain to come back down above the entrance. There were too many arguments going at the same time for me to get a clear dialogue, but the mood was clear enough.

"...should I know? It's not like..."

"...even if he was, there's no telling..."

"...that other student, laughing in the flames..."

"...probably more, I'm certain..."

"...my fault? You filth! How dare..."

I slipped away again, I had heard enough. They were confused and frightened. That was a bad combination for regular people; for psychopath sorcerers, it was a powder keg waiting for a match. They wouldn't do anything for now. It would be a day of whispered discussions and secret agreements. Each would start to make their own plans and start to feel a little more security just knowing that they had taken action. The real fear would start to settle in the next morning.

I didn't go back to camp that day. Instead, I walked the land, hoping to clear my head a little. While I couldn't directly consider the problem, there was a part of me that understood that there might come a time when I needed to make another decision in this story, to come up with another plan. So I put the entire business entirely out of my mind and set my feet to wander. I would be back, of course, the story wasn't over.

I covered a lot of ground, stretching my legs and feeling the ground under my feet. It was deeply comforting to my soul. Walking has always been a form of meditation, not just for me, but for everyone who has ever battled with weighty problems. The great minds behind wars and political movements have often formulated their plans while taking a long walk.

It is an effect that is seldom understood, especially by scholars who get in the habits of holding still while they think, crouched over some book in a library. There is a link between the physical and the mental, and the mere act of walking can stimulate thoughts and creativity more than any book ever could.

Naturally, my purpose in walking wasn't to formulate a plan, but rather to avoid doing so. I walked a wide loop, cutting first down into the open space below the mountains. A thick forest covered the valley floor. Walking through the trees was a little like walking through a maze that had no ending. The view wasn't much, everywhere I looked was just more trees. When someone has nowhere in particular to go, however, a walk in the woods has its own charms.

The beauty of a forest lies in its surprises. The trees would part suddenly, like the tide falling away from the sand, to reveal crystal lakes, fed by cold mountain streams. Other patches were thick with underbrush, the blackened trunks of old trees testifying of a fire that had once ravaged whatever had been there.

When the sun sat high in the sky, I started making a slow curve back towards the mountains, reaching them by late afternoon. I didn't come back where the others were. I found a new canyon and followed it up, anxious animals darting towards caves and overhangs when I startled them. I let my feet carry me higher and higher, always pushing to the next highest point until I turned and looked at the whole land stretched out beneath me.

From this vantage point, I could see across the entire valley, all the way to where another range of distant mountains cut a hazy blue outline into the distant horizon. I decided that when the time came, I would walk to those mountains, perhaps I could see them before the horizons shifted.

There was never any rhyme or reason for when it happened, I had walked full circles around entire planets before the change came. The last couple worlds had been like that. I had spent years walking two lifeless worlds. One had been a desert planet, an empty

170

rock with blowing sand and shifting dunes.

The most recent one had been a ripped landscape of mountains. The planet was very geologically active and the shifting continental plates pushed up mountains and sank oceans as they grated and bumped against each other. Young worlds like that are some of the most beautiful, with vibrant volcanoes and rivers of black stone and glass, but they are also the loneliest, devoid of all intelligent life.

As my feet wandered over the mountains, I let my mind wander back over those dead worlds. It gave great perspective when the night came. Brilliant white stars came out, vivid in the clear mountain air. In the early years of my existence, I had tried to track the stars, to notice patterns or constellations that would help me discern the relative locations of the worlds I walked. After hundreds of night skies, each one as distinct as a snowflake, I gave up.

The stars even had slightly different hues when seen from different places. I'm sure the local residents would all have claimed that their stars were white, but really, the various atmospheres gave the stars cold hints of color, usually blues or pinks. I was a little surprised to note that the stars of this world were truly white.

I walked slower in the dark, picking my way over rocks and across canyons. The sun was almost rising when I finally found myself back in familiar territory. Most people would have found comfort in the familiar, but for me, it was a return to the confusion of this twisted story.

The break had helped. I was able to think clearer, and the sickness in my soul had abated a little. I didn't know if I would be able to interfere in the story again, but I could at least observe without feeling like my mind was going to explode.

I welcomed the clarity as I settled down in the same position I had earlier. In the growing light, I could see Aegon already at the base of the mountain, standing by the poles. How long he had been standing there I couldn't guess, but I appreciated that he was leaving nothing to chance. I doubted he knew it, but the day wouldn't pass without bloodshed.

This time, there was no groggy early riser to alert the others. When the first sliver of sun peeked above the horizon, all thirteen sorcerers moved out onto the outcropping to look below. They moved with all the reverence of a funeral.

As soon as Aegon saw them all together, he raised his hand and set fire to the next pole. He was only slightly more conservative this time, though he still made a show of using more magic than was needed. One more charred post fell to the ground and Aegon again turned and walked back to the woods.

The time had come. I was certain that there were some of them that had suspected the purpose of the poles the first day. Still, they had only been suspicions, dark thoughts to haunt the night. That morning, there wasn't a single one among them who didn't understand.

It was a countdown.

Chapter 21

*Men misunderstand strength. They know that it is
important, so they seek to define it and cultivate it. Inevitably,
they make their definition too narrow, and then weaken
themselves in their pursuit of incomplete strength.*
  –Musings of the Historian

Two mornings, two poles, and three more to go. They would
break now. It was psychology at its darkest. We had already planted
the seeds of doubt and fear. I had already seen it breaking down the
thin threads of loyalty that held the unstable group together. Given
enough time, they might have figured it out, sorted through things
in their minds. With enough time, they might have banded together
again.

Now, with a simple countdown, we had removed all concept
of time from their minds. Most of them wouldn't even trust the
countdown, believing it to be a diversion. It didn't matter whether
they believed it or not, it would make them frantic.

The truly diabolical part was that it was a countdown of
poles and nothing more. I had instructed Aegon to set up the poles
and burn them, one each morning, that was all. There was no plan
beyond that, no attack or subterfuge beyond the mental warfare we

waged against them.

Farmers or soldiers wouldn't have been as affected by such a ruse. Friends would band together and make plans together. I had bet the outcome of the entire campaign on how well the sorcerers had succeeded in twisting their emotions.

Aegon had been right when he had described humans as herd animals. I don't mean that in an insulting sense, but merely as a reference to the strong social instinct that all people are born with. It drives them to form into groups, anything that would give a human a sense of belonging. This social instinct even leads to wars and atrocities as misguided loyalty to a group drives people to put their own group in domination over another.

Humeer and his followers had scorned the importance of this in their lust for power. Ironically, I'm sure many of them followed him initially because they felt a social bond with him. It didn't matter anymore, though. To commit deadly violence against another person is the most grievous sin against the social instinct. That is why killing people was so effective in building their magic, nothing could be more effective at destroying the natural state of mind.

I now used their new strength against them. The natural bonds that would have allowed them to come together as a team were the very bonds they had been spending more than a year destroying. They couldn't feel it, of course,. I it wasn't as obvious as the flames they sought. Even though they couldn't feel it, they were weak. It was the kind of weakness that comes when a person abandons their morals.

I couldn't be in the cave,. N not even I could go there undetected, but I knew well enough where the first break would happen. I worked my way back to the spot above the cave where I could hear what was going on inside. It was quiet, not even the usual whispers and chatter of the previous day broke the silence. Everything that could be planned, plotted, or schemed had already been thoroughly discussed after Aegon's first appearance. Now they were waiting for their moment to strike.

It came in the afternoon, after a silent morning. Two of them started a small argument over whose turn it was to perform some menial task, something the slaves would have taken care of. It escalated immediately, not ten seconds passing from when the first low tones of argument could be heard until almost every voice in the cave was shouting. What came next was inevitable.

Flames burst from the cave opening, a backlash of the terrific heat that had exploded inside the cave. Cooler heads would have realized that a sealed cave was no place for a fire, but someone had decided to strike first, likely the weakest one, the one most scared of being killed off out of hand.

With the first flicker of flame, most of the rest would have unleashed their own magic, either sending it back at attackers or striking out preemptively at those they found to be the greatest threat. I imagine Humeer was a prime target. If we were lucky, he would be among the first dead. Then we could deal with the rest one at a time, separating them from the group and finishing them off in a controlled situation where we had strength in numbers.

Billows of flame and smoke pulsed from the cave opening, echoing the sounds of struggle coming from the inside. It was horrifying to imagine the scene unfolding inside. I had seen what these sorcerers were capable of. Their focused magic would rip through flesh like a hot knife through butter.

If the violence weren't bad enough, the small space would amplify the effects of the flame. The fire would eat up or displace the oxygen in the cave. The sorcerers had created their own oven to burn in. It didn't take long before the grunts and shouts of effort and warning were replaced by cries of pain and the moans of the dying. Civil war had come to the dark sorcerers.

A few of them staggered clear of the cave, coughing and gagging. Those who have never been in such situations can't understand how quickly a body can succumb to the smoke and heat in a confined space. For some, a single breath is enough to make them too dizzy to find their way out. Another breath or two seals their fate. I knew that there would be several who died without ever being burned.

If their comrades had been willing to go back in and drag them out, they might have revived with some help, but the line had been crossed and there would be no going back, no help for the weak.

I was dismayed to see Humeer among the four survivors, hacking and coughing with the smoke, though never once taking his eyes off of the others. Suspicion glowed in the bloodshot eyes. I realized in that moment how things were going to play out.

I didn't like it. Too many had died in the first blow up. My whole plan had depended on an ongoing instability of power, teams and allegiances shifting with each new death. With Humeer surviving, it wouldn't stay unstable for long. There was a problem coming, and I had no idea how to deal with it.

I sat and watched as the remaining sorcerers held their peace talks, right there on the cave ledge. Deals were made and promises given. It was all a lie, and I doubted that there were enough fools left in the pack to believe any of it. Still, it allowed them to work together to get the cave cleared out, throwing the bodies off the edge to roll down the mountain.

They entrenched themselves for the rest of the day. The violence that had occurred had made them much more wary, even though it had come from within. It wasn't hard to imagine that each of the survivors was looking for a way out. They had fallen from godhood in just a few days. Everything that they had taken for granted was suddenly thrown into doubt.

Such was the power of perception.

When all was quieted down, I made my circuitous way back down the mountain and went back to Aegon's camp. Everyone looked up when I entered the camp. Gracie walked right over to wrap me in a lingering hug.

"I worried you might have left us, that it had become too much for you. I'm so glad you're back."

Suddenly very uncomfortable, I returned her hug briefly to reassure her before moving to the fire, breaking off the hug. Still, she sat down when I did and no one was surprised when her small hand found its way to my arm.

"I told them not to worry," Aegon told me. "You wouldn't take off before the story was done, you can't. Just creeping around, being all cold and morbid, weren't you?"

"I have been known to do my fair share of creeping," I smiled. "I go to where the story lives."

"So tell us a story," Matt prompted. "Whatcha see?"

I quickly related all that I had seen up in the mountains. They were an attentive audience and I watched their faces as the key parts of the story were related. They looked hopeful when they heard about the battle, a little sick when they heard how it happened, relieved when they heard how many had perished, and horrified all over again when they heard that Humeer had survived.

"Do you think we could take them on now?" Altur directed his question to Aegon, sensitive as always to my plight. Aegon shook his head firmly. With me out of commission, he was back in command.

"I really envy you, farmer. You can't imagine all the worry I have to go through, having a brain and all. Your life must be so serene not having to see all that I do. Let me remind you that all of us together, with a Historian as a general, barely beat two of them who had already spent all day using up most of their magic. I don't know that we could take down Humeer even if he were by himself.

"Now we've used up our Historian and Humeer still lives. So unless one of you suddenly became a lot smarter in the night, we're going to stick to the plan we have. We've defeated nine of them today, just by burning some useless poles. I'll admit that tickles me, but I'd be a lot happier if Humeer had been among them.

"For all we know, these Historian mind games might finish off some more of them, but we'd be fools to think that Humeer won't be the last one standing if it goes down that way.

"You children had better understand that we have lost our bloodless victory. When the time comes to take Humeer down, some of us are going to die, possibly all."

The camp fell into silence as they accepted the obvious truth he had laid out for them. If I had been able to fully participate, there were still many ways they could have won without losing anyone. Now that I couldn't, they faced an uncomfortable future. At some point, they would stand face to face with Humeer.

Their magic wouldn't be enough to kill him instantly, even if they all ambushed him at once. The reverse was not true. Humeer had the focus to send concentrated threads ripping through them. If everything went wrong at once, he could likely rip the entire party down to the ground in a single cast.

"Tory, any chance you feelin' better?" Matt asked hopefully. I shook my head.

"I've managed to clear my head a little, but I don't think I could give you another plan. I certainly couldn't put myself in the line of fire like I did before."

"Maybe we come up with somethin' and you give us a nod, how 'bout?"

"I might be able to," I considered. I certainly felt better after my walk, but I was still ragged, my soul raging at my transgressions. "I couldn't do it more than once or twice, if I can do it at all. You'd have to pick your moment carefully."

"Better than what we got." He nodded in response. "We'll jus' back off 'til we got somethin' we can all agree on."

Heads nodded around the camp. Gracie gave my arm a squeeze. Even Aegon looked a little relieved, knowing that there might be help in the future, no matter how insignificant it would be.

Chapter 22

In the end, neutrality is a fool's dream. When a person tells a story, they become a part of it.
—Musings of the Historian

"Maybe a little more walking would help," I commented, standing up. Though what I really had in mind wasn't walking, it was another story. My mind had always focused in on stories, and right now I wanted my mind as focused as possible. Gracie moved to stand with me, but I waved her back, turning instead to Matt.

"It's your turn to tend the big fire, right, Matt? Maybe I'll head that way with you."

He shrugged with his usual style and we meandered off into the woods. As expected, there was no trouble at the big fire. I expected Matt to get to work gathering and piling on more wood, but instead he sat down on a large rock and motioned me to sit down at another one close by.

His jovial face had a rare tired look to it. Through this entire ordeal, even with all the sudden changes and hard traveling, his light mood and easy sense of humor had never faltered. Even now, looking on the verge of exhaustion, one could only describe his face as happy.

Naturally, I was suspicious.

I had known a great many people who lived their lives happy. They were warm, giving people, somehow unaffected by life's little brutalities. As near as I could tell, there was only one common thread between all of them, and that was gratitude.

Still, that was not enough to explain Matt. That much happiness, for so long, suggested an underlying driving force. Now that I had cornered him, I was anxious to understand him better. Luckily for me, Matt had a built in sincerity detector. As I had already noticed, his affected accent slipped with his happy façade. As the conversation started, it was firmly in place.

"Wahl, Tory, y' got me out heyah, what you wanna talk 'bout?"

"I'd like to know more about Gracie." Coming at his story sideways like this would have a lot better chance of getting him to open up. Still, it was a dangerous opening move for me. If he decided I was asking questions based on a more personal interest, he would not only clam up, but would likely eye me with suspicion for the rest of the story.

Sure enough, his eyes narrowed a bit as he studied me.

"Why?"

At least he hadn't jumped to an immediate conclusion. That was all the opening I needed to redirect his suspicions.

"I couldn't help but notice that she is particularly skilled with the magic. Now, Aegon and Humeer and that lot gained part of their control through the ravaging of their natural emotions, by killing. Does Gracie have any history like that? I know that's a rough question to ask of you, but I hope you see why I need to know. Also, if it's rough asking you, just imagine how much worse it would be if I asked her."

The suspicion faded from his eyes, replaced by a distant haunted look. He was returning in his mind to the past, exactly where I wanted him to be.

"No, she never got into anything like that. You don't have to worry about her getting all power hungry or anything. It's just not in her."

"Yes, I imagine I already sensed that about her myself. Still, it is odd that she should be so advanced. I understand the two of you left Aegon's school shortly after learning to control the magic."

I left the last bit hanging in the air, using the awkward silence to make the statement a question. He rose to the bait.

"It was her idea. I think she was looking after me. Somehow, it's always seemed that way to me, even though I'm older."

"How long have you two been alone?"

"Wahl, I figger you got me talkin', I 'spose I may as well lay it out proper." His accent slipped back as he smiled at me. I may have guided him along into talking about his past, but I certainly hadn't slipped anything by him. I wondered again at how much intelligence lurked behind those playful eyes.

"I 'spose I better start at the beginnin'. Gracie and me were orphaned pretty early, and it wasn't a pretty sight. You see, both of our parents got the madness."

This was already news. Aegon had mentioned that he had never heard of the madness hitting twice in the same family, Matt and Gracie being the only exception.

"My father got it first. It hit my mother real hard when he

drowned himself. I still remember her beggin' him to stop. Only blessing of the thing was that Gracie was still too young at the time to know what was going on. Our mother carried on for a couple more years, but she was never much good at farming without our father. I helped where I could, but I hadn't even hit my growth yet.

"When the madness came on her, I thought maybe she had suffered for too long. I worked harder to try and ease her work for her. As you might guess, it didn't help. Then came the day when a fit came on her and she hit Gracie. Poor girl hadn't even been doing anything, was sitting by the fire talking to a rag doll. That's when I knew she was gone. It's a hard thing, Tory, I'll tell you that much. To see a person right in front of you, all flesh and blood, and know that they're lost.

"That night I told her the cow was hurt and she went out to see, more from instinct, I reckon. She was still going through a lot of the motions. When she came back, the door was locked. She screamed and raged at the door, kicking and scratching, but I didn't let her in. You see, Tory, there was a window not four feet to the side that I'd left open. If she'd been in her right mind, she could have come right in. I took Gracie as far away from the front door as I could and played a game with her, doing voices and such. She always liked it when I did different voices.

"When the screaming and scratching stopped, our mother was gone. Her footsteps led to the river. We never did find her body, the current was pretty strong where she walked in, I imagine she got swept out to the badlands, like so many others."

I shook my head in wonder at the strength of the boy who had to lock his own mother out to die to protect his little sister.

"It was rough going for a lot of years, but we made it work

and our neighbors helped out here and there. Luckily, we got a good farm. While we weren't able to farm enough to sell or anything like that, there was at least enough to eat for ourselves, even if there wasn't much variety in our diet. That first year on our own, the strongest crop we had was carrots. Boy, I tell you what, a body can get pretty sick of carrots after a couple months of little else.

"We grew up strong together. We really didn't have anybody else. Neighbors were kind enough, but they always acted strange around us, like how people get when you've got something in your teeth and they don't want to mention it and make you feel bad."

I understood the likely reason and offered the explanation for him. "Both your parents had the madness, so they expected you would too."

He nodded.

"The madness is usually pretty random, strikes at people by pure chance, but with both parents getting it, I think that's too much temptation for fate. Turns out they were right, of course."

I pondered this new tidbit of information. I knew of certain genetic traits that could lie dormant for generations, popping up only rarely. Such a thing would give the madness the appearance of randomness, while still running through family lines. Having two with the expressed trait marry and have children before the madness took them could easily have concentrated the strain. Suddenly, Gracie's strength with the magic didn't seem very odd at all.

It occurred to me that Matt had come to the same conclusion, and that was why he was telling me this story, to answer my question. He might not have known about recessive genetic traits, but he was sharp enough to see patterns where others might

184

not.

"Who was first taken with the madness?" I nudged. I already knew the answer, having got a bit of the general timeline from Aegon. But I wanted to hear the full story.

"We got on pretty well for a long time." He continued his narrative while ignoring my direct question. Matt simply did not have the personality to be hurried. "We had each other. You can imagine that neither she nor I had many suitors. Nobody wanted to get close to us.

"I was different from a lot of people who get the madness. Most people spend a lot of time trying to explain their behavior when they start to change. I'd seen it run its full course twice, and I had a front row seat each time. So when I started feeling irritated at Gracie for no good reason, I knew what it was."

"You knew you were going mad?" I asked to confirm. That was truly rare indeed. People who went mad usually had no concept of it, that's what makes mental illness so insidious. He nodded.

"I didn't want Gracie to have to live through that, so I rushed through a lot of preparations and tried to pour my emotions into the work. It's a strange thing, Tory, impossible to describe. Anger you can work out, irritation you can root out by the cause. This emotion just won't shift. You feel it, real as anything, but you can't affect it directly like you can your other emotions. It's like trying to scratch an itch by imagining a rough tree trunk.

"So I left as soon as I could. I was proud to say I never struck out at Gracie. I said a few mean things, but she didn't seem to mind. I think she knew as well as I did. I suspect she also knew I was planning to leave, even though I never told her. She never knew when it would be, so every night during that whole time, she would give me a big hug and tell me that she loved me, like she was saying goodbye, you know? She was trying to make me feel better. By the end, I started avoiding her, but she'd always find me.

"I hit the road, not really knowing where I would go. I brought some food with me, but I knew that people with the madness soon lost the ability to really think through such things and take care of themselves. So I left most everything with Gracie. Figured I wouldn't need it.

"It was some trick of fate that put Aegon and me on the same road. I saw him in the distance and ran him down to yell at him. I had been holding in my emotions so long it all came out in a flood. I started calling him every name I had ever heard my father call our old cow and made up a few of my own. By the end, I was screaming gibberish. It's possible I only remember it that way, the madness starts to twist your memories until you can't remember anything.

"That's certainly the way it was for me. I remember Aegon's face. He wasn't angry back at me, or even insulted that a stranger was yelling at him. He looked more like he had been expecting me, though I don't see how that's possible. I remember he took me with him. I don't remember traveling, and I don't remember most of what happened after that.

"When the haze lifted, I was screaming and choking on smoke and the smell of burned flesh. Aegon was there, but I could only see him as a blurred outline through a screen of heat that distorted everything around me, like reality itself was shaking. I had no idea that the flames were coming from me.

"It took me only a little time to figure out how to manage the magic. I had incentive, you see. Gracie didn't know I was alive. I didn't know what she would do, but I knew it wouldn't be easy on

186

her, whatever it was.

"So I left Aegon alone again. He didn't like it much, or at least that's what I like to imagine, that he was sad to see me go. Fact is, Aegon has always been unhappy about everything. Upset at me going or upset at me staying around, it looks largely the same."

"Ya, not the easiest man to love," I commented wryly. Matt nodded in emphatic agreement.

"In any event, I went back to Gracie. She hovered around me for days, like she couldn't actually believe I was real, know what I mean? She'd lay her hand on my arm every now and again, like she was afraid I'd wander off."

He paused and met my eyes. Whatever unnaturalness people felt when they looked into my eyes didn't seem to bother him much anymore. Instead, I was the one that felt uncomfortable as we shared a moment of understanding.

It was no secret how much time Gracie's hand spent on my arm in the exact same fashion. For that fleeting moment, Matt was just a brother eyeing down a suitor he found troublesome. For reasons I can't explain, I think I loved him all the more for that moment, that taste of normal mortal drama. Then it was gone and he continued.

"When the madness started to come for her, we knew it for what it was, and we were the first people in creation got to feel some sort of hope in the face of it. I'll always owe Aegon for that. We had some time as it grew, so she helped me get ready. We made up a room special for her to wait in while things got bad. She'd sew blankets around thick straw to make pads and I fastened them to the walls and floor so she couldn't hurt herself very bad.

"We also made a chair. It was a gruesome thing, to be honest, but necessary. When we were done with it, it went to Aegon, but I guess he lost it when the school was destroyed. It was sturdy, and with a lot of hinges built in. There were leather straps that could hold a person down. I used soft leather and made the straps extra wide, so they wouldn't cut.

"The hinges were Gracie's idea. She pointed out that sitting strapped in like that would cause sores, so we built the chair so it could move to different positions, shifting her weight around without ever actually having to unstrap her. Near the end, she had to be in the chair almost all the time and I'd change position for her every hour or so.

"Of course, I left her in it one day and went and got Aegon. He'd got another few people unlocked and he was getting better at it, which made me plenty happy, because it was a pretty rough job with me."

Matt paused and pulled up his shirt.

In spite of all my experience, I shuddered a little at the sight. His torso barely resembled a human form at all. There wasn't much of the smooth texture of normal skin. Instead, his chest and stomach looked more like an alien landscape, discolored ridges crisscrossing like mountain ranges. The scars were raised and ugly, making it obvious that they had received no proper attention. Rather, they were left to heal like they were, vicious and open.

I stared. It was rather rude of me, I imagine, but I couldn't look away. By any calculation, there were too many of them. It would be all but impossible for a human being to survive such a mass wreckage of their body. So either Matt was more resilient than almost anyone I had ever known, or…

188

The thought hit me all at once and I took a closer look at the scars. Sure enough, some of them crossed over others, but they had not healed at the same time. That gave me my explanation. The wounds had not been inflicted all at once, like I had seen with Edana. He had been tortured, left to heal, then tortured again.

I felt a tremor of horror as I considered how long he must have been strapped down, waiting for his flesh to heal enough for him to survive another session. I marveled that any man could endure such prolonged agony and still keep hold of his sanity.

Then I considered Matt's ever-cheerful nature and his drifting accent. Perhaps he hadn't kept his sanity after all, at least not all of it.

He put his shirt down and I refocused on the conversation, feeling like I understood Matt a little better.

"Where I'd been able to keep her still for longer and the madness had a greater time to build, her magic unlocked pretty easy. She took to it real natural-like, too. She was the first one besides Aegon to master channeling the fire into a single column.

"We were happy there, really we were. We helped Aegon find and help a lot more people. I suppose he already told you what a great help we were."

He looked to me for confirmation. I could only shake my head.

"Sorry, he didn't mention it."

"Bah!" he scoffed. "Just like that old bugger. We were like his lieutenants, Gracie and me. We would be the ones to go out and gather people, to help him unlock their magic. Gracie did a lot to help refine the process so people didn't have to get hurt as much.

She never did much like that part, you understand."

I understood far too well. Gracie had a deep empathy, she felt the pain of others like it was her own. It was a rare and beautiful quality. I was surprised that she was able to participate so directly in the ugly business at all.

"So why did you leave?" I asked.

"We had that idea the same time, actually, though each of us had different reasons. I had started participating directly in unlocking the magic. I always figured I'd be next in line should Aegon ever kick off, so I figured I should learn it. Well, Gracie didn't like that at all. She didn't much like it that Aegon had to do it, mean old man that he is. The idea that I would have to do it was too much for her. I think she was trying to save me."

I nodded, understanding, and he continued.

"Now, normally, I would have argued a bit with her, but I had my own reason for getting out of there. One of the newer students had taken an interest in Gracie, always hanging around, asking her questions, and playing all nice and sweet. Smart kid, I bet you can guess who I'm talking about."

"Humeer," I grunted, and Matt nodded, confirming my guess. I was surprised at the surge of emotion I felt at hearing this. I recognized the emotion, even though I don't think I had ever felt it before, at least not for as long as I could remember. It was jealousy. I had no right in the world to feel something like that, but I couldn't help but feel a quiet rage at the thought of someone like Humeer creeping around Gracie. Matt apparently shared my disgust.

"He was a curious devil, always prying, always sneaking. Gracie was the most powerful in the camp at the time, except for

Aegon himself. Humeer studied her like a kid studies a fly he's going to pull the wings off of. Worst of all, she didn't seem to see it like that, she didn't seem to mind his attention at all."

Again, the swell of jealous rage, so foreign and unreasonable.

"So the day came when I had enough. I was going to talk to her after dinner that night, suggest we leave and go back to the farm. I was still struggling thinking about what I was going to say to convince her when she out and told me she thought we should go back!

"I hemmed and hawed a mite, so as to make it believable, but you better believe I caved pretty quick."

He smiled at his little subterfuge.

"So we came back. We got the farm put back together and we've been building it up ever since then. We kept to ourselves entirely during the times of madness, so our neighbors never knew either of us had it. From their idea of things, they're still waiting for us to come down with it and drown ourselves."

He smiled at the thought and I couldn't help smiling as well. I didn't see what was funny about it, but when Matt smiled, it made you feel like smiling back.

"So that's the story, Tory." He rhymed it purposefully, again smiling at his own cleverness. "We haven't moved from the farm since; well, at least not until you folks showed up. But now that I've satisfied your curiosity, you're going to satisfy mine."

It was the closest I'd ever heard Matt come to serious intensity. There was not even the slightest trace of accent. I leaned forward and nodded.

"What would you like to know?" I asked.

"Is there anything going on between you and my sister?"

"No, nothing," I replied automatically, giving the only answer I could. Yet, as the words left my lips, I felt the lie of it. I didn't know what there was, but I really couldn't call it nothing. I broke my gaze away from Matt's. He didn't miss the cue and his gaze narrowed.

So it was that I, the greatest liar any world had ever known, was caught in a lie, squirming like a kid caught with his hand in the cookie jar.

"Uh huh…" he drawled meaningfully. "I s'pose I ain't got much to worry about. You gotta leave, right? When all's been done, you're out; I understand that right?"

I nodded, still feeling sheepish. I hoped this would console him, but he only looked more troubled. Still, he couldn't have been that disturbed, as his accent had returned.

"I reckon that's best, but I can't say she'll be happy, and she deserves happiness."

He stood up abruptly and walked away. I sat a while longer, confused at his last statement. I didn't know if he was encouraging me to stay or to leave. This story was so far out of my control, I felt like my head was spinning all the time. I only felt a little better when I was back at the camp, and Gracie's hand was on my arm again.

We all settled down to wait out the day, but it didn't last for long. It was Edana's turn to monitor and feed the bonfire that evening. Altur tried to take her turn for her, but she insisted on going herself. She took his large hand in both of hers, thanking him warmly for his concern. A warm blush rose around his collar and she smiled, turning away and heading off into the woods so he wouldn't see the red beginning to creep into her own cheeks.

She wasn't gone more than ten minutes before she came running back, panic plain on her face.

"There's someone at the fire! He's calling for you, Aegon."

Chapter 23

Once a mind has been prepared, by teaching or experience, it takes only the faintest suggestion to unlock endless secrets.

−Musings of the Historian

"Did he see you?" Aegon was on his feet in an instant, ready for the confrontation he had been expecting. She shook her head. "Are you sure?"

Another shake.

"Is it Humeer?"

"I don't know." He started to make some insulting comment before he realized that she had never seen Humeer. Out of habit, Aegon looked first to me, but turned immediately to Matt and Gracie.

"You two come with me, we'll see if we can't do a repeat of what we did in town. Let's hope it really is just one. I'll approach him first, get him talking, the two of you try to get into a hidden position and I'll try to get to you if a battle starts."

They nodded, accepting his orders as well as his quiet sacrifice, putting himself in the line of fire yet again. Gracie turned to me.

"You'll be there, won't you?"

"Of course, but you know I can't interfere again, no matter what," I warned her. "I'll be there to watch."

"It's enough."

I went ahead of the group to find a good spot from which to watch. It took me a moment to recognize Laigo, the same sorcerer we had seen in town. An angry burn had slashed across his face like a red hot knife, splitting the skin as easily as a razor. He occasionally called out Aegon's name, but not loudly. It was hard to say whether he feared being discovered by someone else or if it just hurt his face too much.

I watched, smiling, as Aegon crept up from behind, placing himself about ten feet behind Laigo. He took a moment to lean casually against a tree before speaking, looking like he had wandered onto a lost child, rather than a deadly snake.

"Looking for me, boy?"

His low tone had the intended effect. Laigo jumped, startled, whirling around to face Aegon. Surprised though he was, he was careful to keep his hands pointed back and down. He had witnessed Aegon burn his partner to death in the village, and he had barely come from the fresh horrors of the day. He wasn't going to take any chances.

"I'm not going to attack you, Aegon." He spoke in soothing tones, like one would do to a snarling dog to calm it down.

"Wouldn't mind if you did," Aegon shrugged. "Might give me something to do with my evening."

He wore his nonchalance like armor. He pushed himself off the tree and walked over to a nearby log to sit down. He made a show of turning his back on Laigo to dust off the log, taking his time to inspect his seat for slivers. The whole time, Laigo stood rigid, sweat starting to bead on his brow. He knew he was being tempted and taunted, and that only made the threat more real in his mind.

When Aegon had finally settled on his log, I could see Matt and Gracie working their way to him, squirming along the ground, commando style. The soft cover of damp leaves on the ground made their approach quieter than the light breeze that wisped through the trees.

"I tell you what," Aegon started suddenly, as if an idea had just popped into his head. He plucked a twig from the ground and tossed it into the fire. "You have until that twig breaks in the fire to convince me why I shouldn't put you down like the sick dog you are."

I felt a teacher's pride as I watched Aegon apply the principle of the ticking clock. Laigo's terror-filled eyes were fixed on the dry twig, already catching fire in the hot coals. He looked briefly to the woods, considering running for it. He realized instantly that he had nowhere to go. He turned and made his case, speaking quickly.

"Humeer sent me out here to scout, try and figure out how many people you had with you and all that."

"No he didn't," Aegon returned. Laigo looked a little sick and nodded. I noted that Matt and Gracie had made it into position, lying flat on the ground, their shoulders twisted to put their hands on Aegon's back.

"I think he sent me out here so you could kill me, that way he wouldn't have to bother with it himself. He and I have never got along. With what happened this afternoon, I don't think I'll live long if I stay around them. I don't have any friends left up there."

"What happened this afternoon?" Aegon's face was a picture of innocent curiosity. "Do tell me what horrible thing has befallen my dear friends. Don't leave out any details."

Laigo's face blanched and he looked back at the twig, already black and charred in the fire. It would break under its own weight any moment. He saw all too clearly that telling Aegon what had happened would cost him time and likely his life. He knew that Aegon knew it too. He launched desperately into his final plea.

"Please, Aegon! You were my teacher once! You can't leave me with those wolves to die!"

"You've done plenty of killing yourself, haven't you?" Aegon's joking tone had turned dangerous. His eyes flicked to the fire right as the twig crumbled, nothing but warm red coals. He raised his hand and a ribbon of fire danced between his fingers. "Time's up!"

"NO! PLEASE!" Laigo was stumbling backwards, his hands raised instinctively to protect his face. He understood now more than ever how horrible a death by fire could be. The ugly wound on his face made sure of that. "I'll help you kill Humeer!"

Aegon sneered, but he lowered his hand.

"Why would I need your help, infant?" he taunted. "It has amused me to toy with you, but this little campout is starting to hurt my back. You've got three days, just like the others. You don't want me to reconsider my merciful position."

"I won't make it three days!" Laigo begged, wringing his hands. "I don't want to die like a dog in the night. You didn't want killing in the beginning, when did you become so cold?"

"An old friend showed me what true power is." I smiled in

the darkness at Aegon's choice of words. "You and the rest of those rejects out there are perversions, failed experiments. I have grown beyond the fire, now it's time to clean up my mess."

"You said you had new students. Couldn't I be one of them, master? I would be a loyal follower." Laigo practically crooned, trying a new tactic of appealing to Aegon's ego.

"You lost that right when you started slaughtering innocents," Aegon responded coldly. I was watching Laigo's face and in the dim light of the clearing I thought I saw the merest flicker of a smile. For all of his simpering behavior, Laigo was a true psychopath, unable to repress the sick joy he felt remembering the murders he had committed.

"Their deaths served to make me stronger," he defended himself. "You can use that strength, I pledge myself to you. Let me live, that's all I ask."

"I'll make you a deal," Aegon muttered, sounding bored. "I don't believe you for a second, but I'll give you some time to prove that you mean what you say."

"Oh I mean it!" Laigo interrupted, pouncing on the scrap of hope Aegon had tossed to him.

"Shut up, you singed whelp, I wasn't finished. You've got three days, just like the others. You can stay here and tend the fire until I need you. If you leave, I kill you. If you let the fire die down, I kill you. If three days pass and I'm unconvinced of your repentance, I kill you. If this seems at all unfair, you are more than welcome to return to the cave and enjoy your last three days in any manner you see fit."

"I'll take the three days, you can call on me for anything, just give me the chance to prove myself."

"Then go get some wood." Aegon dismissed him. Laigo jogged from the clearing, hustling to show his worthiness. As soon as he disappeared into the trees, Aegon hissed to the other two behind him and the three of them took off into the night, going the opposite direction. When they were a decent distance from the fire, they curved back around to their own camp. I met them there.

"Well this is just great!" Aegon fumed, plopping down on a log. "Now we've got a pet snake guarding our fire. The treacherous little weasel would kill us all in our sleep if he thought he could pull it off. I liked it better when they were all in one place and I could keep an eye on them."

"Any chance he was sincere?" Gracie asked from beside me, always the first to hope for the best in people.

"Not a bloody chance! You couldn't see him, but he actually smiled when I brought up killing people. He tried to hide it, but I saw it. He was always a little bit off, the kind of kid who would kick a cat because it was in his way. Under Humeer's gentle tutelage, he's now a raving nut job.

"He's only here because even Humeer sees him as a threat. Judging by the burn on his face, somebody already tried to get rid of him today, probably somebody rotting at the bottom of the mountain right now. You can bet that Laigo didn't wait, probably one of the first to lash out. That was likely all that saved his sorry hide."

"Are we sure that Humeer wants him dead?" Altur jumped in, trying to glean more information without looking ignorant.

"If he were going to send out legitimate scouts, he would have done it yesterday when they were stronger. No, the only reason

Humeer had for sending Laigo out was so that I could burn him to a crisp, maybe betraying some weakness of my own in doing so. He might have even planned on making a getaway during the battle. He might be up there right now, waiting to see bursts of flame from the woods."

"What will he do when there aren't any?"

"It's the Historian's job to tell the future, not mine, you milk sop. There's no telling what he might be doing up there, we just have to wait. Fire watch just became Laigo watch, but keep your distance. I don't mind him knowing that we're watching him, but I don't want him to see anyone besides me. I want to keep as many secrets as I can."

Edana stood to go back on watch. This time, Altur wouldn't be deterred. In the end, they went together to keep watch over the new pet snake. I noted how close to him she walked as they went back into the woods together, their hands almost touching.

An idea came to me, a final gambit that could bring an end to it. It was shadowy and nebulous, especially when seen through the cloud that was my mind. Every time I thought about telling someone, however, the confusion spiked and I could barely remember what I had been thinking in the first place. There had to be a way to tell them,

I went over to the packs and picked up a length of rope. I went back to my log and toyed with the rope, coiling and uncoiling it. I tied a few knots, things I had seen sailors do. Finally, I dropped it at my feet and left it there.

It was subtle, less than a nod, but it still left its mark on my mind. New turmoil seethed in my mind as thoughts turned and tumbled. I hoped desperately that the others had noticed, but I could

200

hardly see straight and felt sick as a dog.

There was a good chance that they wouldn't even take note of my action, and an even better chance that they wouldn't understand it, even if they did notice. It was these uncertainties that allowed me this little nudge. I meant to interfere, and that was enough to trouble my mind all over again, but it was indirect enough that I was able to go through with it.

Gracie was the one who first took note. She didn't actually notice the rope, not at first. She noticed that I was suddenly having a hard time, taking my arm out from under her hand to rub at my head, trying to clear the whirlpool of thoughts.

Her concerned look became focused as her sharp mind worked to unravel the sudden change. Her thoughts finally came to rest on the rope and she leaned over to pick it up.

"Aegon!" she whispered. By that time, Matt was already sleeping, and Aegon was drifting off nearby. Her whispered call brought him around and he glared at her. "Come here!"

He grumbled as he wandered over, still groggy from his interrupted sleep.

"What, what, what?" he mumbled, rubbing at his eyes. He was as grouchy with Gracie as with everyone else, though he never seemed to use insults with her.

"I think Tory wants something done with this rope."

Aegon's eyes shot open, his sleepy mind suddenly alert.

"Did he say something?"

"No, he just went and got this rope, played with it for a while, then dropped it."

"Hardly battle plans, is it? Worthless old madman," Aegon

groused, but now he had the rope in his hands and was staring, trying to divine some meaning from it.

"I know it's not much, but he'd been a little bit better, now he's right back to where he was two days ago."

Aegon's eyes left the rope long enough to peer at me.

"I don't see how you tell with him, but I'll trust you. Any clue what we're supposed to do with this?"

Gracie shrugged.

"I have no idea, but I know he wouldn't have risked interference if it wasn't very important."

"True enough."

In spite of the chaos in my head, I smiled to hear them talking about me as if I were miles away. It was still a long shot that Aegon would figure out my strategy for Laigo based on a prop. Gracie wouldn't be the one to guess, I knew that. She was far too nice for what I had in mind.

Chapter 24

*For the entire history of humanity, we have stared into
fires, hypnotized by the twitch and flow of the blues and yellows.
We see the stars of alien skies reflected in the coals and divine
messages in the dance of the flames. Fire is magic.*
    –Musings of the Historian

The next morning came soon enough. I had taken up what
was now my usual spectator position, seeing everyone, but visible to
no one. Humeer was already on the ledge when the sun broke over
the mountains, the two other remaining sorcerers flanking him to
either side. Somehow, seeing three of them united was more
intimidating than the clustered throng.

They talked quietly among themselves, wondering why
Aegon wasn't at his usual spot. Their eyes darted around as they
talked, wary of an ambush. A horrified gasp escaped the sorcerer at
Humeer's right as Aegon broke through the tree line.

Laigo walked a few paces in front of him. A rope was tied
around his neck in a loose loop. Aegon holding the other end
completed the image of a leash. Laigo's stumbling gait and hanging
head completed the perfect image of a beaten pet.

When they got to the poles, Aegon jerked on the leash,

pulling Laigo to a halt. He snapped a command that wasn't quite discernible over that distance. The leashed man obediently raised his hand and sent a thick band of fire to encircle the next pole, the heat from his concentrated flames reducing the entire pole to ashes in moments.

Aegon smiled broadly up at the waiting sorcerers at the cave. It was the kind of smile that could be seen for miles, equal parts of cheer and smugness. He tugged on the leash again and the two of them soon disappeared back into the tree line.

I wondered idly how long it had taken to convince Laigo to go through with it. The psychopath wouldn't have much use for dignity, he wanted power and he wanted to live. He had thrown in with what he saw as the stronger camp. In his mind, little humiliations to weasel his way into Aegon's trust would be a small price to pay.

Aegon had successfully guessed my intention, though I doubted he knew what the effect would be. He was a man of firm convictions and a tortured soul. He was very clever in his own way, but his idealism made it impossible for him to truly think as Humeer would.

It was human nature, people assumed that other people thought the same way they did. It has always served as an unintentional mirror for those who knew where to look. Cheaters always assume that everyone is trying to cheat them. Liars assume no one tells the truth. Most relevant to this case, killers expect violence and traitors never trust anyone.

It had taken most of the night for me to calm down after my small hint to Aegon. I knew I couldn't do much more. I couldn't even warn them of the violence this latest tactic would unleash. Unless I had missed something vital in my confusion, there were people here before me who wouldn't see another sunrise.

Humeer and the other two disappeared back into the cave. I waited hours for some sort of reaction, but the cave sat as silent as a grave. Finally, my curiosity turned to the camp in the woods. I worked my way back down into the woods. I passed by the bonfire first.

Laigo sat on a log, staring into the fire, lost in his own schemes. The leash was gone. It didn't matter, the rope had only been a bit of theatrics, but it had been effective.

Having seen Laigo, I started circling around to find whoever had been tasked with keeping an eye on him. It didn't take me long. I hadn't even completed one full circuit around the camp before I came upon the watchers.

They were all there, I was surprised to note. Not only were all five of them watching over Laigo, but they had packed up the entire camp from the looks of things. The packs leaned against trees, ready to hand. Matt jumped when he saw me, but breathed easier when he recognized me.

"How'd you get so close, Tory?" he hissed in a low whisper. They weren't that close to Laigo, but nobody was taking chances.

"Long practice," I whispered back. "Longer than you can imagine."

He nodded, his eyes widening slightly as he considered the full implications of what I had said. Aegon moved and took me by the sleeve, pulling me away from the group and further from Laigo's camp. When we had moved a sufficient distance into the woods, he turned so we could talk.

"I know you can't do much here, but I figured you'd want to get caught up on the story. Maybe it will help if the time comes when you can help a bit again. I'd love to know why we did that this morning, but if all I've got left from you is a bloody nod, I'm not going to waste it."

"Makes sense," I agreed, though I wasn't sure if I even had a nod left in me. "So why is everyone packed up? Are you moving out?"

"No chance of that, I imagine," he grumbled. "The way things sit now we'd likely be worse off than ever if we quit now. We packed up because of your bit with the rope, which I'm only hoping I got right."

"Why would you pack up because of the act with Laigo?"

"Because whatever that meant, it's probably going to set the ball rolling again. That means that something is going to happen and we might need to move quickly, no time to pack up."

"That's very clever."

"Altur's idea," he admitted grudgingly. "He said you wouldn't have put yourself through all that for something small. He argued that if it was something big, as it likely was, it was going to shift things; and when things shift in this group, it means fire, battle, and death."

"It's a decent argument," I offered, not denying or confirming anything. He nodded, getting my meaning.

"I had to agree, as much as it pained me to side with that flea-picking dirt grubber. That's also why we're here watching Laigo. I figured that when things started to pop, we'd either need his help in a hurry, or we'd need to kill him in an even bigger hurry."

"He's a dangerous man," I stated simply.

With nothing left to say, we made our way back to where the others waited. They weren't actually all watching Laigo, they weren't quite close enough for that. They were close enough to move in and attack, if it came to that, but one of them still needed to work their way closer to actually see him clearly. By chance, I had happened upon them in the middle of a change. When I got back, Altur was gone, keeping watch. The others lounged silently, there was nothing else to do.

I settled to the ground, happier to wait for the coming storm with Gracie's hand on my arm. For all my expectations, the day passed calmly, the changing of the guard the only interruption to the monotony. My instincts raised the hairs on the back of my neck.

There was no way Humeer would let this slide, it wasn't his way. There would be an attack, I was sure of it. With the sun already dropping below the mountains, it looked like it would come in the darkness. It was going to be a night of treachery.

I hadn't been trying to warn them in any way, I didn't think I could, but Gracie was suddenly studying me intently.

"Aegon!" she hissed. Like the previous night, Aegon wasted no time hurrying over to peer at me along with her, like I was some grotesque insect he was studying under a magnifying glass.

"Did he say anything?"

"No, he hasn't done anything, but he's uncomfortable, anxious."

"He looks fine to me, bored even."

"No," she insisted, her whisper insistent. "Something's wrong and he knows it, he just can't warn us. Whatever we're doing, it's not enough. Something's coming."

Aegon sat looking at her for a long awkward moment, turning things over in his mind. Finally he waved to the others, bringing them in on the council. It was Matt's turn on guard, but Edana and Altur crawled over to listen, their eyes wide and scared. It looked like I wasn't the only one who felt the danger hanging in the night.

"What's going on?" Altur asked.

"Gracie here thinks that our resident Historian has got himself all worked up about something."

"Gracie would know," Edana stated firmly. I wondered what she meant by that.

"I have to agree," nodded Aegon. "What are we supposed to do about it? If any of you dirt clods has any clue what we should be reading into a Historian's indigestion, I'd love to hear it."

"We're already watching Laigo," Altur offered. Aegon rolled his eyes.

"Your grasp of the bloody obvious never ceases to amaze, farmer, care to offer anything helpful, or are you just happy to be here?"

"He means that if there's danger coming we're unaware of, it's probably coming from them in the cave. Even a great magician like yourself should have seen that." Edana put a hand on Altur's knee as she lashed back at Aegon, defending her husband.

"That's likely so," Aegon fired back. "But that doesn't do us a lot of good, does it? We can see Laigo because he's standing around a bloody big fire. We can't see those in the cave and we don't dare get closer to check.

"I'll definitely buy that something might happen tonight, but either they're going to run away or they're going to attack. If they are running, we don't dare follow and leave Laigo behind, so we'd have to deal with him first. If they're attacking, there's almost no way we can see them coming anyway. What would you have me do?"

"Look," Gracie cut in, "I don't think Tory would be this worked up over them running in the middle of the night. I think we'd do best to assume that we're going to be attacked tonight. So what would they do? We can think our way through this, Tory has carried us far enough."

"Fine, though I'll have to take your word that your precious Tory is all worked up, he still looks fine to me. I suppose if they were going to attack tonight, they would try to take us by surprise, so they might try to sneak up on the fire."

"Maybe we should warn Laigo," Edana suggested. "If they come upon the fire, they'll find him first."

"If they truly are attacking, he might be their main target," Aegon mused. "Thanks to our little charade, they might consider him the only one they can kill right now. They might be looking to take him out before we can teach him how we came to be impervious to their magic.

"We have a fine line we need to walk here. I don't mind the idea of him being taken out, especially if we don't have to do it. Still, if we warn him first, he might be able to do them some damage at the same time."

"So let's warn him," Altur prompted. He was committed to the course, and he knew that meant killing all of the dark sorcerers, but his personal honor rebelled at the thought of leaving anyone to die by ambush.

"All right then, the rest of you stay out of sight. If they're sneaking up, there's nothing saying they aren't already coming up on us. Everybody get down and stay quiet. Run if they find you. We can't win this in a stand up fight. Historian, I imagine you're coming."

I nodded and stood. I wouldn't be influencing the story, Laigo had already seen me, knew I was with Aegon, and coming along would give me a front row seat as this next chapter began, likely the last.

Laigo stood as soon as we entered the clearing, his eyes widening as he recognized me. I understood all too well. The last time he had seen me, I had my head rocked back, laughing cruelly as their fire poured into my body. He took an unconscious step back.

"The time has come!" Aegon announced. "We believe that Humeer and whoever's left will be coming down to kill you tonight."

Laigo's face paled at the thought. Instinctively, his eyes flicked to the woods, his mind going over his retreat possibilities. If he could get rid of us fast enough, he might be able to get a decent head start. Aegon read his expression easily.

"Yes, you could do that, might even be your best chance to live through the night, but it still doesn't give you any more than the two more days you've got. You might outrun Humeer, but you can't outrun my friend here, he doesn't even sleep."

Laigo looked back to me, trying to weigh his fears. He had already seen me stand in the flames. By now he was sensing what the others already knew, that I wasn't truly part of their reality. Even regular people sometimes caught on when they looked too closely into my eyes. There was something there that didn't fit, something unnatural.

"Do you have a plan?" he asked hopefully. Aegon snorted loudly, laughing out loud at the ludicrous thought.

"You poor dumb puppy, do you want to hear my plan? My plan is to sit by and see if you are actually willing to stand and fight for the right to be one of us. When I'm good and convinced, or when you're dead or run off, I'm going to kill Humeer, his boys, and whoever else I feel needs killing. How's that for a plan?"

Laigo's eyes again went to the woods, he looked truly miserable. I knew that if he stood and fought, there would be no relief. Aegon couldn't and wouldn't save him when the time came. No matter which side won, his fate was sealed. Still, knowing how many innocents he had slaughtered to enhance his power, I could feel no pity for him.

"I suppose I don't have…" Laigo choked on his words suddenly, throwing himself in a hard roll to his right. Aegon didn't wait to see what had spooked him, he ducked and jumped towards the woods, just in time to have a lance of white flame burn past the spot where he had been standing. Not hitting anyone, it hit into a tree on the far side of the clearing. The tree burst into flames under the searing heat, adding even more light to the bizarre scene that unfolded in that lethal night.

Chapter 25

Battles waged in daylight are fought by soldiers. Battles waged at night are fought by savages.
-Musings of the Historian

For the first few moments of the battle, everything was silent as the parties tried to find each other in the darkness. The crackling of burning wood was the only sound. Aegon had made it easily into the trees on one side of the clearing. Laigo, using the bonfire to mask his movements had made it to the other end of the clearing.

It was possible that he would try to run, but he had to know that his chances weren't very good. If what Aegon had said was true, he was the primary target and he had lost his shot at a head start. Most likely he would decide that his best chance for survival lay straight ahead. All he had to do was fight and survive long enough for Aegon and me to enter the fray.

What followed was a terrifying game of cat and mouse. I only caught glimpses of movement in the trees as the players moved around like pieces on a chess board. It didn't take long for someone to make a mistake.

There was a loud crack, like someone had stepped on a dry branch. Instantly, the scene exploded with light as one of the other sorcerers cast a bright arc of fire, cutting across the trees at about waist level. Only the best were at play now, and the arc of fire would have cut anyone who had been caught in its path nearly in half. Every tree it had hit was now on fire, but the attack hadn't hit anyone. It had only served to betray the attacker's position. An answering salvo came sizzling back at the other sorcerer.

The stab of flame did not come from where the noise had been, it came from above. Laigo had apparently climbed a tree, then threw a rock or heavy stick down to draw the others out. His simple deception had worked and his aim was true. His mass of fire ripped into the other sorcerer. The silence of the night was shattered by his death cries. Laigo shouted his triumph, too caught up in his bloodlust to exercise good sense.

It was at this moment that the key flaw in his plan was revealed. The tree made a great platform for an ambush, but it didn't leave him much of a retreat. Another attack of flame was on its way before Laigo was done exulting over his small victory. He dodged away, trying to use the tree as cover. It was only partially successful, as the trunk wasn't quite wide enough. He cried out in pain as the flames licked at his exposed arms.

I could see the attacking sorcerer now, Humeer's final remaining companion. I still hadn't seen Humeer yet and I knew why. I had left only one conclusion for a mind like his, and he would hold back until the right moment. Still, I couldn't see it lasting much longer.

With Laigo tucked behind the tree trunk, the other sorcerer couldn't make his killing shot, though he could wound Laigo's arms at will. That wasn't good enough, though, and he didn't dare put himself in a position where Laigo could fire back at him.

The obvious tactic finally occurred to him and he lowered his attack, focusing the flames on the lower trunk and branches. He was going to smoke Laigo out, force him to reveal himself. As the branches below Laigo caught fire and the smoke started to engulf him, it looked like things were nearly over.

"Now, Aegon!" Laigo yelled. He was a clever little snake, that was for sure. If Aegon actually listened, he would be saved, but he wouldn't be counting on that. The aim of his little ruse was made immediately clear when the attacking sorcerer started looking frantically around the woods, expecting an attack.

That moment was all Laigo needed and he pushed himself off the branch. It was a mix of falling and climbing as he bounced his way back down to the ground through flaming branches.

He threw himself to the side, desperately seeking cover. His body was covered with burns and bruises, his left arm hanging limp at his side. The cloak of darkness was largely gone now. The fires had spread and we now found ourselves at the center of a budding forest fire.

The whole night was lit up by the violent conflagration and it was only getting brighter. It was also getting harder to breathe as the fire spread and used up all the oxygen in the air. I hoped that Aegon had the sense to stay low to the ground.

There was one more thing, one more piece that needed to fall into place in this little puzzle. As the last sorcerer stalked the wounded Laigo, I saw it. Humeer appeared in the flickering flames, silent and creeping.

Once again, we had managed to turn their strength against them. Once again, the humanity they thought was weakness would have saved them. The week had put fear in them, and the fear had turned to treachery. Parading Laigo around in front of them had been the last straw for Humeer. He would see betrayal everywhere. Every friend would now be an enemy waiting to strike.

A man as intelligent as Humeer wouldn't leave such things to chance. He would strike first, looking to remove Laigo as a threat before things got worse. Beyond that, Humeer could no longer trust his own men, any of them.

He had kept himself out of the battle because his paranoia now saw all of them as combatants, as likely to fire at him as anyone else. He had unleashed his minions to fight amongst themselves, wearing down their magic as they killed each other.

Now, as the end spiraled closer, he would move in to finish off whoever stood as victor. It was surprisingly similar to my own plan for them. He couldn't afford having men that powerful around, men who could almost match him in magic.

The battle between Laigo and Humeer's last sorcerer was short but intense. Laigo was wounded, the pain making him disoriented and shaky. He tried to account for this by spraying his fire in broad arcs, thrashing side to side, trying to dodge any incoming strikes. The other sorcerer had to jump quickly to dodge the incoming ribbons of white heat. He didn't jump quickly enough and he went down hard, his leg failing him as a blast of fire seared his knee.

In a roar of anguish, the sorcerer sent a wall of flame rushing over Laigo. The snake of a man fell backwards, smoke and steam rising from burnt flesh and clothes. The life wasn't out of him completely and he raised his own hand to counterattack. Nothing came, he had used all of his magic too quickly in the battle.

The opposing sorcerer dragged himself closer, laughing to

himself in spite of the pain of his ruined leg. These men may have been saved by Aegon from the madness that would have made them kill themselves, but Humeer had led them to a new madness that destined them to kill each other.

With his eyes on his victim and anxious for a final victory, the sorcerer never thought to look back, never had a chance to see Humeer, who was now walking calmly up behind him. The roar and crackle of the flames all around them meant he didn't even have to creep quietly.

The sorcerer propped himself up against a tree, using his good leg to push himself into a semi-upright position where he could look down on the burnt Laigo, who was spitting curses at him from the ground. A single ribbon of flame was enough to silence him forever, a flash of light and done.

His victory was short lived, as Humeer raised his hand to end what he had started. Aegon's greatest student smiled as he sent a small ball of flame into the back of the other man's neck. Death was instant, the attack concentrated, intense, and efficient. He took a moment to smile down at the two corpses, a devil glorying over his angels amid the flames of a burning world.

He turned to leave. My guess was that he would head further south into the valley. He would have decided that he needed to find something he could use as leverage against Aegon. Until he knew more about Aegon's newfound powers, he would have to exploit his old teacher's humanity to insure his safety.

I moved, making my way silently around the outside of the clearing as Humeer walked through the center, The bonfire was suddenly a small light compared to the burning trees he left in his wake.

In one of those moments where fate gambles with tragedy, Aegon stood up right as Humeer came near to his hiding place. It hadn't been intentional, that much was obvious. Aegon had been hiding behind a large deadfall, the old mossy log keeping him out of sight. I guess his curiosity had proven too much when all the shouts had gone silent.

It would be hard to say which man was more shocked when their eyes met, barely ten feet away from each other. Their astonishment did not quell their instincts, however, and they both struck and dodged at the same time, sending spears of fire at each other as they threw themselves sideways.

Humeer, the younger man, was a little faster and got out of the way of the flames, the heat sizzling by above him. Aegon, still a little slowed down by the healing wound on his ribs, was struck full in the chest by Humeer's cast. The blow knocked him backwards, his dodge turning into a full sprawl. He hit the ground hard and didn't move.

Humeer rolled smoothly to his feet, immediately darting through the trees, trying to anticipate Aegon's next strike. It took him a minute of this before he caught a glimpse of Aegon's legs among the leaves. His dodging stopped and his movements became deliberate, leaning carefully out from behind a tree to get a better look, disbelief clear on his face. He worked his way closer, still using the trees for cover.

Finally, convinced that the danger was past, he stood fully and walked over to where Aegon lay.

"Where is your new magic?" Humeer whispered, barely audible over the crackling fire. It wasn't a taunt, as one might expect, but an earnest question. His mind was still trying to cope with the confusion he felt. He leaned down and felt at Aegon's neck for a moment. He spoke louder.

"You are one hard man to kill, I'll give you that. You should have listened to me, master. We could have been gods together. Why couldn't you see it? You caused all this destruction, not me.

"Your school, your teachings, they were all meant for greater things, why couldn't you understand? All those other students, my friends; I couldn't allow any of them to live then, and I can't allow you to live now."

Humeer sounded truly sad. This was what made him dangerous. Men like Laigo hungered for power, knew full well the evils they were willing to commit to gain it. But for all their deception and treachery, men like Laigo could never begin to approach the totality of someone like Humeer. He was a true believer, a zealot convinced of his own righteousness.

A manipulator or power hungry warlord might pause at times to consider the consequences of his actions, to weigh things in the balance. It took someone who believed himself a saint to commit true atrocities without hesitation and without a look back. I could see it now in Humeer's eyes as he stood over his teacher, believing himself a savior as he raised his hand to finish Aegon.

Chapter 26

Every sacred moment is made that way by sacrifice.
–Musings of the Historian

Flames leapt, but not from Humeer's hand. They came from the woods. Matt threw them in an impossibly long cast for someone of his experience. The crew had come to help when they heard the battle and saw the flames. They were badly out of position when the time came, however, having headed first to the far side of the clearing, now burning and abandoned by all but the dead.

Matt, being the closest and the fastest, had cast a ball of flame, too wild to be effective, but enough to distract Humeer from his coup de grâce. Humeer dodged easily. His return stab of flame was surgical, lancing though the woods to strike Matt in the chest. Just like Aegon, Matt went down hard, his body and mind unable to cope with the explosive heat.

Gracie was right behind him and moved off to the right as she ran in, casting fire of her own, pulling Humeer's attention away from Matt and Aegon. Humeer sent tiny stabs of magic after her, careful to conserve his magic now that he faced multiple opponents.

He was unable to hit her flitting form as she danced her way through the trees. The same agility that saved her, however, also made it impossible for her to level an accurate counterattack, and her own magic did little more than set trees on fire. She lacked the laser-like control of Humeer, so her attacks were broad gouts of yellow flame.

It was at that moment that I saw Altur, crouched low to the ground, sneaking up behind Humeer. The lights from hundreds of fires danced on the shiny blade he carried. It was nothing more than a dagger, something a farmer would carry in his belt, but it would be enough to end Humeer if he could get close enough.

My heart caught in my throat as the second stroke of bad luck came crashing down. Intent on his target, Altur did not look down at the ground he was crossing. He was within two paces of Humeer's exposed back, his massive shoulders already tensing for the final lunge. His foot came down on a thick dry branch and it cracked under his considerable weight.

The loud snap penetrated the night, heard easily even above the crackle and roar of the growing fires all around. Humeer spun, panicked, casting a broad sweep of magic around himself as he turned. The thick wall of flame caught Altur coming in and tossed him backwards. Luckily for him, it had been a mass of heat, cast in panic. There was none of the white heat that came from a focused strike.

Altur was burned deeply, but very much alive, and he scrambled backwards in the thick leaves trying to get clear before Humeer could hit him again. He was so close that Humeer didn't even have to use his magic, he leapt forward, aiming a kick at Altur's back, sending him sprawling.

"Am I now to be attacked by these worms, these cattle with no magic?" Humeer fumed as he stalked up for a finishing blow. I

220

could hear Gracie's frantic footsteps as she tried to get back in the battle, but she had been focused on leading Humeer away and she was too far away to save Altur.

Appearing from nowhere, Edana leaped onto Humeer's back, scratching and clawing at his face and throat like a wild thing. Humeer cried out and stumbled backwards under the ferocity of this new onslaught, trying to shake her off.

Humeer finally managed to grab a hold of one of her arms and tried to yank her off, but she clung to him like a barnacle. Enraged, he roared and licking flames appeared around his fingers as he sent magic burning into her unprotected arm.

Her cry of pain split the night as smoke hissed from her arm. It was Humeer's last bad decision. Edana's magic was still wild and untamed. Her magic broke free with her scream as her whole body lit up with furious licking flames.

Humeer screamed then too, as the body clinging to his started burning at him. Frantically, he sent more magic into her arm, trying to burn her free like one would a parasite. A fitting analogy, as the natural flow of magic transferred his own magic through her and back at himself. A cycle of searing destruction.

The more energy he poured into her arm, the more poured right back into him. The final victory came as a simple matter of placement. He could only burn more and more magic into her arm which was charring under the inferno, but her own fiery arms were wrapped around his head and neck.

His dying throes only sent more magic through Edana into himself, a short circuit conduit of magic and fire. It all ended at once, Humeer dropping to his knees, finally releasing Edana's arm to clutch at his ruined throat. He held that pose for one eternal moment, frozen forever in my memory. Then he toppled forward onto his face, never to move again.

Altur was at Edana's side in an instant. They made for a curious pair, each overreacting to the injuries of the other. Really, it took quite a bit to overreact, as their wounds were quite severe. Deep burns covered every bit of Altur's exposed skin. His eyebrows were gone and already his flesh was beginning to blister. When I got close enough, I couldn't help but notice the intense smell of burnt hair and roasted flesh.

Edana's injury was just as serious, if not more so. The place on her arm where Humeer's hand had been was burned black, the imprints of his fingers seared deep into her arm. I knew at a glance that she would never have full use of that hand again. Tendons and nerves would be ravaged by a burn that deep. If the flames hadn't cauterized the wound, she might have lost the arm entirely.

Gracie was to them almost as soon as I was, worry in her eyes.

"We have to get out of here," she commanded. A glance around showed she was right. The fire in the trees had been spreading. The far side of the clearing was already a roaring inferno, a fitting funeral pyre for the last of the dark sorcerers. Fortunately, there wasn't much wind that night, but the fire would spread outward and intensify. To stay here would be death.

Altur nodded and turned to where Aegon lay motionless. He gathered the bitter old sorcerer up in his arms like one would a sleeping child and followed after Gracie. She led all of us to where Matt fell. The fire hadn't quite spread to where he was yet, and it took a moment to find him in the dark.

"Matt?" His sister called to him, her voice breaking from the emotion.

"I'm here, Gracie," he responded. His accent and playful tone were completely gone, his voice scarcely more than a whisper.

"Hold on, we'll get you out of here. Altur, do you think you could bring both of them if you dragged them? We only need to get clear of the woods."

"I'll make it happen," Altur assured her and started to lay Aegon back down. Matt was already shaking his head.

"No need for that, big fella." His voice was even weaker than it had been mere moments before. "I'm done, Gracie, got a bloody... big hole... in my chest."

"Please no," Gracie's eyes brimmed with tears as she held her brother's hand and begged him not to die.

"Nothing for it." He spoke in gasps now, three or four words at a time with long ragged breaths between each set. "It's a wonder... still alive... you there, Tory?"

"I'm here."

"You really never die?" It was only airy whispers now, and I answered in kind, the moment too fragile for more than a breath.

"Never."

"You ever forget?"

"Never."

"See Gracie... I'll live forever... Tory'll remember... he'll tell everybody... I'm a hero." His smile was warm and goofy, the old Matt back for one vital moment. Gracie cried, tears running down her face as she sobbed.

"You were always a hero, Matt."

The smile was still on his face, but the eyes were vacant now.

Whatever had made Matt who he was had gone. Gracie held his hand and sobbed, her back shaking with the force of the emotion inside her. The growing warmth on our backs left little time for mourning. She turned to me.

"I can't leave him here. I know what I'm asking of you, but would you carry him for me?"

I nodded, hoping I was telling the truth. I was surprised to find that there were tears on my face as I leaned down to lift the limp body from the ground. I was no longer any kind of observer in this story.

Matt wasn't a character in a story, he was my friend.

Surprisingly, it didn't take much from me to scoop him from the ground, becoming part of the scene once again. I suppose I wasn't influencing the story all that much by carrying him, his story had ended with his heartbeat. Perhaps I only suffered by affecting the living.

We made our way clear of the woods, but no one felt like stopping. We made it all the way to the river before we finally stopped. There was no making of a camp. Altur rolled out a blanket for Edana and she settled down on it.

He started to set out another blanket for himself but she grabbed the corner and pulled it to her, bringing him along. She didn't speak a word, just pulled him to the ground and laid her head on his chest. They stayed that way the whole night, though I could never tell if they were sleeping or not. Likely not, considering the pain they would both be in.

Gracie waited until I had settled on the ground until she came and took up her place at my side. There was no hand on my arm that night, however. She wrapped her arms around my neck, plunged her face into my neck, and cried.

She cried for hours, her hot tears running down her face and onto my shoulder. When she ran out of tears she just held me, quaking like a leaf in the wind.

Chapter 27

If there is one thing sadder than unrequited love, it is shared love that cannot be.
—Musings of the Historian

The morning sun dried tears and ended the horrible night once and for all. With the first red rays of morning, Gracie left my side and got to work. Besides myself, she was the only one of the party who wasn't injured. She threw herself into setting up camp, starting a fire for breakfast and hauling water from the river to help cool fiery wounds.

Aegon had survived, but barely. The fire had hit him in the chest, but in a glancing blow. It was as if a flaming sword had been swiped across his ribs. The damage was deep and I wouldn't have been surprised if his lung on that side had been damaged. At that, I wouldn't have been surprised if he died anyway. Men who endured that kind of agony often did.

He looked strange, lying there like that. His face was pale, but peaceful, a sharp contrast to the angry wound a mere foot below. It was hard to believe that this vulnerable, innocent looking old man could be the same sarcastic tyrant that we all knew.

Altur started the day with a long bath in the cold river,

clothes on and everything. He was the only one whose wounds looked better in the daylight. True, he made for an interesting spectacle with most of his hair burned off and his skin burned as red as a cherry, but it hadn't blistered as much as I had expected and nowhere was it bad enough to be life threatening. I even suspected his eyebrows would grow back normally.

Dripping wet and feeling much better, he helped Gracie with the chores of the camp. Soon everyone was fed and had their wounds treated. There wasn't that much that could be done. Edana's arm still bore the ugly char marks of Humeer's hand. When she tried to move her fingers, she found that her last two fingers wouldn't move at all, and her thumb could only manage a slight twitch. It gave her hand the distinct look of a curling claw.

I held Aegon's head as Gracie spooned tiny amounts of broth down his throat, careful not to choke him or interrupt his troubled breathing. Once everything was taken care of, the decision was made to go back to Altur and Edana's farm, it being the closest.

We only had to camp in the open one more night before we found ourselves back at the farmhouse with the golden fields laid out in front of it. It seemed like years since I had first seen it, though I knew it had only been little more than a month. Altur's handiwork displayed like a signature around the farm and everything was still in good working order.

The next couple of days were a blur. We buried Matt there on the first day. There wasn't much ceremony to it, only a solemn sadness as we lowered his body into the ground. Gracie didn't cry then, all her tears had already been spent, but she clung to my arm like a drowning person.

A day later, some of Altur's blisters burst and became

infected, making him sick and feverish. Edana insisted that he take her bed and get some rest. Feeling a bit like a peeping tom, I made my way around the house to watch as she tucked him in. There was one more thing I wanted to see from this story.

She helped him with a long drink of water and dabbed at the blisters with a cool cloth. I knew enough about medicine to know that there wasn't a serious problem, just a small fever that would likely pass in the night, but she insisted on hovering over him.

Finally, her fussing over with, she leaned in, pausing only for a moment. The uncertainty passed as she looked into his eyes and she closed the remaining distance between them, bringing her lips to his in a lingering kiss.

The shocked look on his face was priceless, but the broad smile that followed was enough to warm any soul. Their second kiss was even longer and deeper, not the kind to end any time soon. I left the window then. I had seen enough.

I was glad that I had moved away, because Gracie came around the corner of the house moments later.

"Aegon's awake!" she announced. "He's asking for you."

I was to the front door and into the house as fast as I could move. The innocent victim I had seen before was gone. Aegon was back and the pain of his wound screwed up his face like he had been sucking lemons.

"You get over here, you lifeless pile of horse dung," he commanded. He breathed the insults like some men muttered prayers. It was his way of coping with the pain. "Unlike you, I don't have all eternity to waste away, I have one pig foot suck of a life and I am done wasting any more time with Historians. Is it over?"

"Yes, it's over. Humeer and everyone who followed him are dead. The secret of power through murder is safe with people who will keep it."

He nodded, his chest relaxing as if the news had eased his pain.

"Did I do it?"

"No, it was Edana in the end, she attacked him when he was about to kill Altur."

"Well doesn't that just figure? That's the luck of the stupid for you. If that dumb farmer ever dies it's going to have to be by my own hand, I see that now. What else?"

"Matt died. He saved you by distracting Humeer, but he had to put himself in the open to do it. Edana and Altur both got burnt pretty badly, but they'll be ok, better than ok, really."

"I am sorry to hear about Matt. He was one of the best men I've ever known. It takes a special sort of strength to turn away from power like he did. He never showed it, but he was strong, could have been stronger than all of us if he had pursued it."

His sincere praise of Matt was made all the more powerful as it wasn't his way to speak well of anyone, ever.

"I suppose you want me to thank you for getting us through this, but we had a deal, that's all."

"I understand. I am truly happy that things turned out as well as they did."

He stared at me for a moment, studying. His expression softened.

"You know," he started quietly. "I think I actually believe you. I'll hold up my end of the deal, but trust me when I say you won't like it. Are you sure you want to hear this?"

"I'm sure."

"I guess even Historians can be fools," he grumbled. "Here goes, but don't say I didn't warn you. I can't tell you who it was did this to you or who set you on this course. I can only relate what the last Historian told me when he remembered his name and his story.

"He told me something that has stuck with me ever since, I hear the bloody words in my dreams. He said 'I walked a thousand lifetimes to learn wisdom; then I walked ten thousand more to learn fortitude.'"

"Fortitude?"

"Did I stutter? Yes, he said that even that was hardly enough. When the memories came, he was barely able to withstand them. I have seen things that would curl your hair in my troubled life, Historian, but I have never seen more horror in anyone's eyes than I saw in his as he remembered."

"What kind of things could have happened to him that he needed ten thousand lifetimes to cope with them?" I whispered, feeling a little horrified myself.

"You've got it all wrong, friend. It wasn't things that had been done to him that burned him up inside..."

The old man shook his head, sincerely sorry to share this last truth.

"...it was the things that he had done."

"The things he had done?" I parroted dumbly.

"Oh yes, he described things to me that I could hardly imagine. He told me of worlds crushed, entire races obliterated at his hand. Wisdom came easily enough, the time and the stories he witnessed showed him all the virtues and humanity a man could ever wish for. When he knew his own story, his soul burned with the guilt of it. I think if he had been able to die, he would have pulled a mountain down on top of himself to make it happen."

My mind reeled at the implications. If what he was saying was true, and I had no reason to doubt it, my time as a Historian was not a thing of fate or chance, but a kind of purgatory that I was passing through. All that awaited me at the end was a mirror to show me my own depravity. My mind rebelled against the thought.

"Surely you can't think such things of me!" I protested. "I have a hard time believing that I could even be capable of anything on that scale."

Aegon scoffed, though the action caused him to wince with pain.

"You see everything all laid out before you, the lives of us mortals, but you can't see yourself. You took down a veritable army of powerful sorcerers with nothing but our rag tag band of misfits.

My stomach twisted as he laid into his explanation, showing me my own actions in unforgiving clarity.

"You manipulated people, played with their minds until they murdered each other. You even used our own emotions to move us around as easily as a child's playthings.

"You can't believe that all of those strategies came from your stories. You can't imagine that someone else would have been able to twist people as effortlessly as you did. Not one person in a billion has that kind of power inside them and you did it with your hands tied. You did all this and you did it in barely more than a week."

I knew he was right, but he wasn't done yet.

"Think of what you could do if you had years. Think of what you could do if you had magics or technologies. Imagine what you could do if you had armies, Historian."

I was immune from every disease, but at that moment, I felt sicker than any victim of any plague. The world spun around me as I was suddenly made to face what I had done. Just days before I had stood and judged Humeer, the man who slaughtered people, thinking himself justified the whole time. Could I really be like him? Could I be worse?

Aegon reached out a feeble hand and laid it on my shoulder.

"I never thought I'd say this to a Historian, but I'm sorry. I know that you've got horrors ahead of you. More than that, I'm quite sure you deserve them, every last one of them. My Historian was a monster beyond any nightmare's scope and I suspect he wasn't in your league. Still, I feel sorry for you all the same."

I gripped his hand, accepting his support silently. I didn't trust myself to speak.

"You'll be leaving now," he stated simply. "You won't be able to stop it now that you know that I'm going to live. The story is finished."

I nodded again as Aegon spoke what were usually my lines. I could already feel the desire growing strong within me. Now I recognized it for what it was, compulsion. Aegon gave my shoulder another squeeze and lowered his hand back to the bed.

"Goodbye, Historian, and thank you."

"Goodbye, Aegon," I mumbled and walked out into the bright sunshine. Gracie was there waiting for me. Her smile at seeing me died when she saw the look on my face. Somehow she knew.

232

"You're leaving, aren't you?" Her voice was quiet. I nodded. "Can't you stay? Don't you want to stay?"

I realized at that moment that I did. I wanted nothing more in all the worlds and eternity than to stop here, to spend my life in peace. I wanted to stay with Gracie.

She saw the tears in my eyes and moved to embrace me. For the first time, I hugged her back, holding on like she was my anchor, but the storm would carry me away, I knew that.

"I do want to, but I can't." The words ripped from my throat. "I have to follow this through to the end. I have no choice."

"I understand."

Looking up at me suddenly, she ran her fingers into my hair and made a fist, a clump of hair in each hand. She pulled my head down and before I knew it, her soft lips were on mine. She held me there, holding me close in a long kiss. I couldn't say how long it was, but it ended.

That kiss ended me. The compulsion was upon me now. I had made another move in this story, made it my own in the most extreme way possible. My vision failed and my mind was a hurricane of molten blades. I squeezed her one last time, but even the feeling of her was fading, lost in the maelstrom.

"I'll remember you," I promised. "If I live another million years, I will never forget you, Gracie."

Looking back, I wonder at times if I actually said the words. My memories of that time are chaotic and the final moments are a mix of impossible images and sounds. I could not even say for sure if I walked away or if the horizons shifted then and there. All I knew was that my next clear memory put me in a new land, under new stars.

I was walking.

My journeys had a different feel after that, I knew that every step was one step closer to the end. I knew more than I did before. I knew that I would face horrors before it was all done, I would have to face whatever demon I carried somewhere within.

Still there was a kernel of hope in my quagmire of bad news. I knew now that I had, at one time, possessed great power. It had been enough to attract the attention of beings even more powerful; powerful enough to send me on a journey of ten thousand lifetimes.

Perhaps power such as I wielded was enough to push back the walls of time and chance. Perhaps I could find a way to return to that time and place I yearned for. It was a fool's hope that I could return someday, to feel Gracie's hand on my arm again, but I had been far too wise for far too long. I would hold to my fool's hope.

You may understand now. You might begin to see through my eyes and know how hard it was for me to tell this story. You might even wonder why I would choose to share such a story when the telling of it causes such pain. What you must understand is that this story was more than just a story. This story is important. This story was not about me.

This was a story about you.

235

About the Author

Lance Conrad lives in Utah, surrounded by loving and supportive family who are endlessly patient with his many eccentricities. His passion for writing comes from the belief that there are great lessons to be learned as we struggle with our favorite characters in fiction. He spends his time reading, writing, building lasers, and searching out new additions to his impressive collection of gourmet vinegars.
For more from the author, follow him online at:
Website: lanceconradbooks.com
Twitter/Instagram: @LanceConradlit
Facebook: www.facebook.com/LanceConradLit/